MATHILDA'S

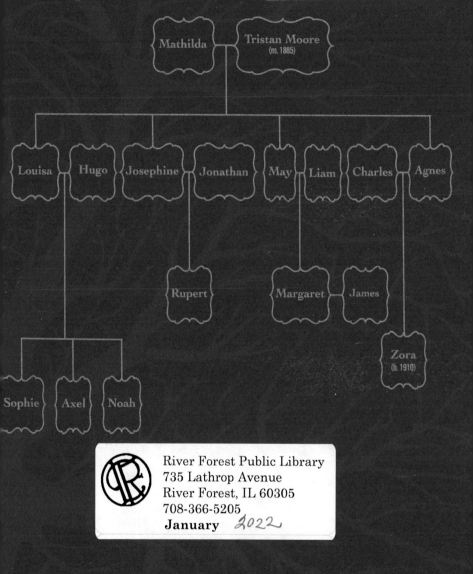

Mathilda — Tristan Moore (m. 1885)

Louisa — Hugo — Josephine — Jonathan — May — Liam — Charles — Agnes

Rupert

Margaret — James

Zora (b. 1910)

Sophie — Axel — Noah

SHATTERED MIDNIGHT

A MIRROR NOVEL

DHONIELLE CLAYTON

HYPERION

Los Angeles   New York

First Edition, October 2021
10 9 8 7 6 5 4 3 2 1
FAC-021131-21232

Printed in the United States of America
This book is set in Century Gothic Pro, Citrus Gothic, Cochin, New Old English/
  Monotype
Designed by Marci Senders

Library of Congress Cataloging-in-Publication Data
Names: Clayton, Dhonielle, author.
Title: Shattered midnight / by Dhonielle Clayton.
Description: First edition. • Los Angeles ; New York : Hyperion, 2021. • Series:
  The mirror • Audience: Ages 14–18. • Audience: Grades 10–12. • Summary: In
  1920s New Orleans, eighteen-year-old Zora, banished after an incident in Harlem,
  struggles with her overbearing family, magical powers, love of jazz, and forbidden
  romance with a white man.
Identifiers: LCCN 2020057036 (print) • LCCN 2020057037 (ebook) •
  ISBN 9781368046428 (hardcover) • ISBN 9781368046435 (paperback) •
  ISBN 9781368070942 (ebk)
Subjects: CYAC: Magic—Fiction. • Family life—Louisiana—New Orleans—Fiction. •
  Musicians—Fiction. • Jazz music—Fiction. • African Americans—Fiction. • Love—
  Fiction. • New Orleans (La.)—History—20th century—Fiction.
Classification: LCC PZ7.1.C594725 Sh 2021 (print) • LCC PZ7.1.C594725 (ebook) •
  DDC [Fic]—dc23
LC record available at https://lccn.loc.gov/2020057036
LC ebook record available at https://lccn.loc.gov/2020057037

Reinforced binding

Visit www.hyperionteens.com

To all the great love stories shattered by history

AUGUST 1928. NEW ORLEANS, LOUISIANA.

New Orleans was a place people went to disappear. Maybe it was the sticky heat, a thick cloak wrapping you up and never letting go. Maybe it was all the peculiar people swelling the French Quarter day and night, easy to fold into and hide. Maybe it was the never-ending jazz music—trumpets and tubas and sharp pianos—luring many down cobblestone streets and into alleys, never to be seen again. Or maybe...just maybe...it was all the dead folks buried aboveground and the whispers about the Crescent City being a crossroads town, a place where unseen worlds kissed.

That was what Zora had figured out in the two months she'd been living here with her aunt Celine—who had agreed to hide her because she'd gotten into a pile of trouble back home in New York City. She thought maybe this was why her mama sent her down here in the first place. Zora wasn't even her real name, and she still hadn't gotten used to answering to it. But she'd wanted . . . *needed* . . . to vanish. Arms, legs, and feet fading like a pencil sketch erased from a notebook so no one would ever know what she did back in Harlem.

"Mama said you're supposed to be trying on that dress so she can fix the seam before dinner," her cousin Ana snapped. "Everything is about the fit, you know." Willowy and small, Ana twirled before the family's full-length mirror in the bedroom they all shared, leaning in to inspect the new freckles she'd gotten since the start of the summer.

"She's too busy staring out that window again," Ana's sister, Evelyn, replied, sitting at the vanity and fussing with her tight curls. They were barely a year apart yet seemed like twins. A deep blush pushed through her rich brown cheeks. "Always gawking like you never seen nothing. You're from New York City—you've seen *everything*!"

"There's another parade," Zora answered, eyes still glued to the train of bodies, the ginger cat in her lap also perking up to look out the window. She loved the bright parasols and how the blasts of trumpets sent ripples across her skin. The beat of a distant drum mingled with the clash of cymbals and the squeal of trumpets. She tapped the beat on the sill. The jazz here was different than at home: a little wilder, a little less tidy, a little more unpredictable. Each evening, she felt like she was part of it all, the melodies of the parades; rhythms and timbres and crescendos of sound she'd never heard before captured her full attention. She'd fall asleep to the sound of music and revelry somewhere outside the window.

This was the best thing about this city so far. The constant music. The constant dancing. The constant frivolity. The way even the cobblestones seemed to hold rhythms and rumbles. People said jazz was born in this peculiar city. And she could believe that. Her heart reached for the songs, shaking loose something deep in her bones, the thing she wanted to hide.

Evelyn craned over her to see outside. "That's a second line. We do that when someone dies. Just wait until Mardi Gras. The parades will be happening for weeks. People on stilts, floats, and all the masks to look at."

"The krewes will try to outdo one another," Ana added. "We won't be able to sleep. It'll be terrible. I'll have bags under my eyes again. By the time February comes, I'll have a permanent migraine."

"You don't have parades in New York City? You're supposed to have it all," Evelyn scoffed.

"Most folks are too busy working," Zora replied. "If you danced in the street, you would get flattened like a hotcake by a taxi. But there's some." She continued. "Like on St. Paddy's Day. Or a ticker-tape parade, if someone important visits. Mostly for white folks."

"I can't believe Mama gave her the nice one." Evelyn held up Zora's party dress, and the golden beads and silk chiffon caught the sunlight. Celine, a dressmaker, had made it just for Zora. Evelyn ran her plump fingers over its drop waist. "One of the best Broussard originals to date."

"You can have it." Zora turned back to the window. "I'd rather stay up here, anyway."

Ana snatched the dress from Evelyn. "But she's our guest for a little while," she mimicked, putting on her mama's thick French accent. "But she's had it rough. . . . But she's here to convalesce. . . . But she has a *strange affliction.*"

Zora had gotten used to them ganging up on her. The insults had frayed her nerves when she'd first arrived, scraping across her skin like sandpaper. Now she let the words drift out the window to be swallowed by the big brass melodies. She had to.

"What happened in New York? You never did tell us," Ana pressed for the thousandth time, as if that would make Zora suddenly change her mind and spill the whole story.

"I don't want to talk about it."

"You never want to talk about anything," Evelyn spat back. "It's been two months and you won't even tell us about what it's like to live in New York. We're cousins. We're supposed to know things about each other, and we don't know squat."

"I'd rather—"

"Be playing the trumpet," the two said in unison.

"Or the bass guitar. I can play that, too. Even the trombone," she barked back.

Their frowns deepened.

"That's why your lips are so red and puffy. Mama says women have no business playing brass. You'll look like a dried-up fish when you get old," Evelyn said. "Mark my words."

Ana chuckled at Evelyn's barb. "You can't mope around forever," she said, and blew a kiss. She pointed at Zora's house clothes—the simple blue cotton dress Zora loved. "You better get dressed. Mama set up this dinner for you to meet all the important people. Miss Annabelle has to like you. Did you know that the Original Carolina Krewe only accepts the best?" Ana did a twirl across the room to make the beads on her dress click-clack. "The boys fight over who courts you first."

"I don't want to be a debutante." Zora sucked her teeth. Before the accident in New York City happened, she'd planned on becoming the most famous female jazz musician who ever lived. She was a quadruple threat. She could sing, act, dance, and play any instrument she touched. She'd show the men that women were just as good, if not better. "It's fussy and silly, if you ask me."

Evelyn gasped.

"Lucky nobody did," Ana shouted back.

Zora sighed as her cousins listed out all the things that were wrong with her for not being excited. If they knew—*really* knew—what was truly wrong with her and what she'd done, they'd scream and cower in fear. They'd get her aunt to kick her out into the streets. They'd look at her like a monster.

And maybe they'd be right.

Even now, she could feel the hum of her gifts just beneath her skin, like the vibration of a song she used to love. One that felt like her own little secret. But now she hated it.

As the last of the second line eased past the house, a young white man paused. He wore a boater hat, had a face full of freckles, and stared through the window with a strange, clever grin. He looked too perfect and put together to be standing on their corner. He didn't belong. Zora sat up straight, a jolt up her spine. They made eye contact. He lifted a tentative hand and waved.

The bedroom door snapped open. Aunt Celine pounded in, her heels making the floor tremble. Zora's ginger cat cowered and tucked himself deeper into the nook beside her.

With thick dark hair pulled into a perfect chignon, Aunt Celine was a passé-blanc, her skin the shade of steamed milk sprinkled with almond powder. Her aunt pursed her lips in disappointment, and she clapped. "Girls, didn't y'all hear me calling you? I don't holler for my own health." Her honey-colored eyes narrowed, inspecting each of them. "Why aren't any of you dressed? The Colliers and the Bechets will be arriving any moment. I need you downstairs to flash your pretty smiles and remind them that the Broussards throw the best parties in the back-a-town. Mabel is setting out the oysters already."

"Our *houseguest* doesn't want to come," Ana reported with a smug grin.

Before Zora could get a word out, her aunt stomped over and grabbed her arm, yanking her from the small nook, the only spot she felt comfortable in this house.

The cat screeched.

"Get that creature off my furniture. Didn't I tell you about cats? Bad luck. Count your blessings I don't have it stuffed." She tightened her grip. "In the Broussard household, we don't turn down perfectly good invitations to parties thrown in our honor."

Zora tried to wrench away. Her heart fluttered wildly, a humming-bird trapped in her chest, as her aunt's manicured nails dug deeper into her flesh.

"Glad you felt it. Something to knock you out of this rut. You've been skulking around like you can't do nothing."

The warning signs flickered: the flash of heat through her, a thunder beneath her chest, a crackling across her skin as if lightning were about to strike. It hadn't always been like this. She let her eyes close. She only had a few more hours, then she'd be outside and engulfed in music—*just* music, the kind that healed instead of hurt.

Stay calm, she whispered to herself. *Stay calm*.

Her aunt scowled. "What's wrong with you, baby girl? I don't know what my cousin let you get away with in New York City, but this ain't the Big Apple, and you best start acting like it."

Zora's eyes snapped open. She gritted her teeth and blinked back tears.

Evelyn and Ana hid satisfied grins behind their hands. Zora felt bruised. The mention of home usually flooded her with memories: a summer Sunday in Harlem, taxis honking, newsboys running up and down West 125th with the latest, the Apollo's lights spilling stardust on the sidewalks, the grocers sweeping and chasing children away from their storefronts, the folks sitting on stoops playing cards or trading gossip when it got too hot inside their apartments . . .

But that was long gone because of what she did. Now the memories were crowded out by the sounds of falling bricks and cracking wood, the snap of broken bones, and the roar of fire mingled with piercing screams. This woke her every night.

"Mabel said you sent her away earlier. It's your turn for a bath. Don't make me have to come back in here, because I'll be bringing a switch. Eighteen is not too old for a good lashing."

Zora flinched.

"You hear me?"

"Yes," Zora mumbled.

"Yes, what?"

"Ma'am. Yes, ma'am, I heard you, and I understand."

"You better." Aunt Celine pulled an envelope from her apron pocket. "This came from your mama. Maybe it'll help set you straight. I told her how you've lost the good sense the Lord gave you, that's what. How lucky you got it, to have kin to take you in when things get rough. Should be more grateful—and gracious...."

Zora stammered out an apology. She didn't want to disappoint her mama. She took the letter and traced her fingers over the looping cursive.

"None of that funny business, you hear?" Aunt Celine sucked her teeth and waited for Zora to nod before turning to her daughters and inspecting them. "Ana and Evelyn, wipe all that off your cheeks. This is *not* the Tenderloin. Come with me. You need to entertain our guests as they arrive." She attacked their cheeks with her handkerchief, then strutted out, leaving behind the heat of her words and the scent of her cloying perfume.

While the housekeeper, Mabel, drew her bath, Zora retuned to the window nook. The young white man in the hat was gone.

She unfolded the letter.

August 15, 1928

My dearest,

I miss you so very much, my little love. Your aunt Celine as always full of complaints and commentary. But she's just a honeybee—no real stinger. Give her a few flowers and make her feel like the queen of the hive, and she'll leave you be. She's not much different than the women I cook for.

I wish you were still home with me. And I'm sorry I couldn't prepare you or protect you from this. I'm the one to blame. I should have told you more.

But don't worry—like I said at the train station, the veil is complete. No one will ever know what happened with Mrs. Abernathy, and no one will be able to find you. Not as long as I live. I promise.

I'll take a peek in on you. But you cannot write to me. Try to forget about us for a while. Tell others who ask that we are gone. You are gone, in a sense. You're Zora Broussard, and you're not my little girl anymore.

This storm shall pass. I have faith. Cling tight to the music. It is both a blessing and a curse, but you must use it.

We will be all right. You will be all right. I hope one day we will be together again.

Love,

your mama

Zora held back tears. What would her white German grandmother think if she could see Zora, her Black granddaughter, now a fugitive in New Orleans? What would she think of the gifts that she'd taught Zora so little about, of what Zora had done with them? What disappointment might Zora see in her eyes?

She was a murderer.

She was a monster.

All because of magic.

2

hen Zora was very little, in their Harlem brownstone, magic was as normal as the jars of spices on her mama's kitchen countertop, folded in like butter in biscuit dough. She'd pick up her father's horn and play a tune, and clusters of notes would flutter in the air as if they'd been lifted from the bars and lines of a music sheet. They also leaked out of her when she'd use her magic, her conduit. Anything she wanted to move with her mind would be swarmed with those ladybug-size notes and carried away.

One day, Oma sat in the small apothecary room, where she mixed tonics for neighbors. She took a lily and placed it in Zora's little hand. "Try," she'd challenged little Zora.

Zora had squeezed her eyes shut, clenched her teeth, and imagined the flower changing color with all her might.

Oma had chuckled. "Liebling, remember the music. Sing me the song your papa always plays on Sundays."

Zora's eyes lit up, and the happy lyrics burst out of her. And as they did, the soft petals of the lily turned crimson.

Oma smiled. "Each one of us has magic that comes most easily. The one that rises to the surface like cream on fresh milk. Mine is potions—potions that help others and that helped me live so long and give birth to your mother and aunts.

"Your mama's is food—she can enchant a kernel of pepper, make dirt taste like the most divine chocolate. But yours . . ." Oma continued. "Yours is music."

Zora remembered how much fun it had been using her magic as a little girl. Pointing tiny, fat fingers and moving her dolls. Floating spice jars over bubbling pots on the stove, adding a pinch of salt and a dash of cayenne to the simmering liquid under her mama's watchful eye. Clouds of music notes transformed into trays lifting fine china and cast-iron skillets as Mama pulled her latest pie from the oven, blowing over it to cool and enchant it with love and luck. It felt like a stream of melodies flowing outward from her heart, helping her mother make her glorious creations.

And then, just after Zora's seventh birthday, Oma died. Her mother forbade her to use the magic anymore. Said it made her feel too sad. Said the magic could be used against them if they were ever found out—they could be hunted for it.

So Zora had thrown herself into becoming a serious musician. Her soul demanded it. Her truest joy. She buried the magic deep inside the best she could, letting only the notes soar out of her. But the magic buzzed right behind them, waiting, wanting out.

And now she knew just what it could do if she wasn't careful.

"Your bath is almost ready, sugah," Mabel called out.

Zora bit her bottom lip. Watching Mabel's round bottom bent over the tub, she hummed the tune she'd just heard outside. The notes leaked from her fingers like tiny drops of blood. The sensation felt like uncorking a shaken champagne bottle, the magic eager to rush out. The drops stretched into strings, then looped around her mama's letter in a protective ribbon before carrying it to the bed.

She loved knowing that the magic was still buzzing in her veins, a reminder of Oma. But it also felt like a sharp memory of what she'd done back home, what she was capable of.

"I put a little lavender oil in the tub, baby. Gonna be a long night.

Need a little calm 'round here." Mabel stood in the doorway, hands on her hips, a smile lighting up her brown face. The warmth of her voice always felt like a quilt ready to swaddle Zora. It was like Mabel understood how badly she needed kindness.

Zora kissed Mabel's cheek and went into the bathroom. After a long soak, Mabel helped her squeeze into her dress and sprayed her with enough rose water that even if she sweated in the heat, no one would ever know. She eased down to the dining room and lurked beside its double French doors, clutching Oma's cat to her chest like a shield she hoped would protect her from whatever would happen in that room. She'd successfully avoided all her aunt Celine's parties and attempts to fold her into the colored high society of the city so that maybe by the beginning of next year she'd be ready for debutante season. But everyone had headaches from the Louisiana heat. Everyone had upset stomachs from the rich food. Everyone was a little homesick at first before getting adjusted. Her excuses had run out.

Laughter escaped from behind the doors and Zora could feel the thick electricity of conversation even from her hiding spot.

She stole a glance into the room. The chandelier twinkled over a long table set for ten. The best china had been washed and laid out beside the silver she'd seen Mabel polish during breakfast. The piano sat in front of a large window, its stark white and black keys begging to be played. Everything shone under the chandelier, and even she thought it would make her look cleaner and prettier than she ever had. Aunt Celine only liked beautiful things in her house.

Zora took a deep breath and stepped into the room. Evelyn cleared her throat, and Ana snickered. The table was full of well-dressed people who reminded her of perfect little brown dolls in matching sets—husbands and wives and their pretty children.

Aunt Celine stood. "Let me introduce my niece, Zora Broussard. She might be rude and late to every party, but she's very pretty."

Zora flashed her best smile. A trail of sweat skated down her back. Another group of people to meet and charm. She would need to make the best impression so that when debutante season started, she'd be accepted.

She still hadn't gotten used to these sorts of folks—fussy and nosy, with a comment for everything. She missed how no one paid her much mind in New York City. Here, she lived under a microscope, her every move up for scrutiny, always woefully failing.

Dr. and Mrs. Bechet sat closest to her aunt, looking like plump figurines atop a wedding cake. Their two sons gawked. Mr. and Mrs. Collier and their son wore ridiculous matching pinstriped outfits and sat sandwiched between Ana and Evelyn. Zora felt like she'd entered a circus masquerading as a dinner party.

"Zora, have you lost your tongue?" her aunt chided. "Say hello. And did you bring that animal down for dinner? Nobody wants cat étouffée, honey." Her aunt grinned at everyone, and chuckles rippled through the room. She walked over to Zora, grabbed her arm, dug her nails into her skin, and whispered hard in her ear: "I thought we discussed no cat outside of your bedroom. Now send it back upstairs and put a smile on."

Zora put the cat on the floor and sent him back upstairs to her room before turning to face the group. "Hello... I mean, hi.... Um, good afternoon," she stuttered, and a flush of embarrassment warmed her cheeks.

"She's come all the way from New York to spend some time down south and away from that noisy place. Though I suppose New Orleans also has quite a bit of ruckus," her aunt added.

The men at the table rose from their seats and waited for Zora to take hers. She eased into a chair beside Evelyn. "I'm sorry it took me so long."

"I told them all how despite being from New York City, you move slow as cane syrup," Aunt Celine said, earning raucous laughter.

Zora grimaced, biting down on her lip to stop a rude remark from slipping out. Mabel wheeled out a spread—fire-red crawfish étouffée, jambalaya bursting with shrimp and sausages, red beans and rice, a steaming cauldron of gumbo, and a pyramid of biscuits.

"It's magnificent, Celine. Truly. You didn't have to go to all this trouble," Mrs. Bechet remarked, her pretty eyes large and wide as she inspected the food.

"Trouble is my middle name on Sundays. And I aim to spoil."

"Must've been holed up in the kitchen," Mrs. Collier added.

Aunt Celine showed her three old oven burns on the inside of her forearm. "Kitchen battle scars."

The look of the thick brown stripes sent a chill up Zora's spine. When she closed her eyes, she saw the ones on Mama's arm, and the buried anger shook itself loose. She swallowed with a gulp.

"Something wrong?" one of the Bechet boys asked Zora. He had the light mustache of a man, but a young boy's squeak still lingered in his voice. His mother called him Jean-Claude.

"No," Zora said, clipped.

Ana and Evelyn guzzled the fizzy champagne their mother let them have on special occasions. Even with prohibition, New Orleans seemed to always be fully stocked with wine and liquor if you knew the right people.

Mrs. Collier spoke the world's longest prayer, and Zora thought the food might turn cold before she was done with all her *amen*s and *hallelujah*s and *thank you, Lord*s.

Aunt Celine lifted her glass and toasted. "To a new season of gloves and gowns and good fortune."

Zora was in desperate need of that. A new fortune. A new start. Everyone took bites of the delicious food, oohing and ahhing and giving Aunt Celine praise even though Mabel had made it all.

"It's never too early to prepare for our debutante season. Before you know it, November will be here, then Christmas, and then New Year's and Mardi Gras. So much to do. It's only August, and the stress is showing up in my shoulders," Mrs. Bechet said.

Mrs. Collier nodded as Aunt Celine hummed in agreement.

"Zora, tell me, does New York City have as many rats as the papers say?" Dr. Bechet asked, his raspy voice booming.

A series of chuckles followed. His wife playfully slapped his arm.

"As many as I've seen here in the French Quarter. Also, you have more cockroaches than any city should. They even fly here. It's very odd and unfortunate." Zora felt her aunt's hot gaze as she spoke.

"Touché, touché. Those pesky water bugs cling to these streets. I swear they'd survive the End Times." He rubbed his salt-and-pepper beard, and his nose crinkled, making Zora brace for another rude question. She gripped her water goblet, taking a nervous sip.

His delicate wife, Mrs. Bechet, flashed Zora a pitying smile, a crease of worry appearing on her forehead. "What do your folks do, Zora?"

"My mama's a chef."

"A cook?" she replied.

"No, a *chef*. She took classes at the only culinary school in all of America. Up in Boston," Zora responded without thinking, puffing out her chest. "And she's worked with many famous chefs."

Aunt Celine flapped her fan aggressively. "She's very, very, very talented," Zora continued. "Always in the papers for this or that. She'll probably be famous one day for whipping up a biscuit that can melt in your mouth and not leave anything on your hips."

Laughter rippled out all around the table.

"Everyone loves her pies and cakes. They can make you forget your own name," Zora boasted, but then swallowed, remembering her mother's warning in her letter about distancing herself from them . . . and what happened.

"Wonder what she'd think of our Louisiana cuisine. It's a mix, like the people who live here and made this fine city. I've done my fair share of traveling, and I swear, there's nothing like a good pot of gumbo and a king cake," Dr. Bechet said.

"What's a king cake?" Zora asked.

A chorus of gasps exploded across the table, followed by more laughter.

"Junior"—Dr. Bechet turned to his son and winked—"you'll have to show Zora around and make sure she gets the best slice from Mama Sugar's Bakery."

The young man nodded, dabbing sweat off his glistening forehead. "Yes, sir," Christophe Jr. said.

Dr. Bechet licked his spoon. "Celine, teach this girl about our ways down here *and* how to make a good étouffée. You put your foot in it, I must say."

"Mabel made that," Zora grumbled under her breath. "All of it."

"What was that?" he asked.

"Nothing," she replied. "Nothing at all."

Her aunt shot her a burning look, the threat of severe punishment in her gaze. Maybe if Zora showed her aunt that she was a terrible dinner guest, she'd let her stay in her room next time. Maybe she'd give up this fool's errand of turning her into a stuffy, boring girl to present like a gift box to eligible men. Maybe she would write her off as hopeless and leave her be.

Stay calm, she told herself. If she made it through dinner, she would have her reward. It wouldn't be much longer.

"If she wants to get married down here, she'll have to learn, too. To be a good wife, one needs to know one's way around the kitchen," Mrs. Collier added.

"I don't want to be a wife—good or bad." The words slipped from Zora's mouth before she could catch them.

Her aunt's gaze turned into a scowl. Her cousins hid their giggles behind fans.

"She has peculiar ideas," her aunt said. "Don't mind them. This good Louisiana air will fix her right up . . . and some good old-fashioned Southern home training."

"I just mean—I mean—I'm not so sure," Zora said.

Mrs. Bechet pressed a hand to her chest, elegant nails tapping her pearls. "Marriage is a sacrament, petite. It is our divine lot—the thing women must do to ensure God's children are brought into this world." She turned to Aunt Celine. "I see you need more of the Lord's word in this house."

"Trust me, Adele, we have plenty. That sinful city she came from teaches young women that they can gallivant around and neglect their duties. But not down here. We still have Jesus. She will walk the righteous path one way or another."

The table exploded with chatter about how Zora might not have been raised right with the church at the heart of her household and how her marriage prospects would no doubt suffer from this neglect. They blamed New York City. They blamed the 1920s jazz and too-short skirts and the fast fancy women in old Storyville and loose morals. They blamed alcohol even while sipping their bootlegged champagne.

Then they blamed her mama and daddy.

She could no longer keep it all in. The calm left her, and the little bit of magic she'd let out earlier rushed forward to her fingertips, releasing a high, ringing pitch. The glass in her hand turned midnight black before it shattered.

The women at the table screamed. The young men gawked, mouths ready to lure flies.

"Jesus Christ Almighty!" one said.

"How'd that break?" another replied.

Aunt Celine leapt to her feet; horror and distress marred her beautiful face. "Zora has a mighty grip is all," she said. "She will be excused. Her constitution is still adjusting to our rich food." She swept Zora from the room, and as soon as they were out of earshot of the party guests, her voice dropped an octave. "I told you about funny business. I'll have none of that in my house. You hear me? Not one bit." She lifted her rosary and kissed it, then dug her vial of holy water out of her pocket and sprinkled it over Zora. "I warned you. This is the last time. The little money your mama and daddy are sending me is *not* enough to take on this burden. Now—out of my sight."

Zora dragged herself back up the stairs, hearing her aunt's excuses trailing her up the steps.

"Her grip is extraordinary.... It's from my cousin—her father— who taught her to play the trumpet. Though we all know that girls should not be using those kinds of instruments. Makes hands and mouth indelicate. Strong like a man's. Unladylike. Very, very much so."

Zora's cat greeted her, rubbing his long ginger tail along her leg.

"Another mistake," Zora told him. "Made a pile of trouble again."

Her heart felt sore with disappointment. When she'd first arrived, she'd tuned and played her aunt's piano, hoping music would make her feel a little closer to home. But her cousins made remarks about the types of women who played jazz music, and thick notes poured out of her like torrential rain, choking the room, knocking the portraits off the walls and toppling the lamps. Aunt Celine had a fit. She swatted the notes out the windows like flies, and Mabel ran around in hysterics trying to sweep up broken glass and set objects upright. Her aunt forbade her from singing or using any instrument in the house.

She didn't understand. It wasn't the *music* that was to blame.

The cat stared back with huge sea-glass–green eyes and led her to the window nook. She had so many questions and so much anger about the fact that she didn't have the answers. Why had Mama refused to let her use magic all these years? Was it because she knew deep down it was bad? Why hadn't she told her anything about it?

Everything was just so unpredictable and off-kilter after what happened with Mrs. Abernathy in New York City. Now it all rushed out violent and sharp as Mama's chef knives, and she had to focus on staying calm so she could control it.

The moon rose outside the window. Zora stuffed pillows beneath her blankets and arranged a silk headscarf in the shape of her head. Her cat sat on the mound to keep watch as she arranged everything into a familiar form.

"Good job." She kissed his wet nose and pulled the sheer bed curtains closed. They would not only protect that lump from mosquitoes, but from the prying eyes of her cousins and aunt. *This* stomachache would last all night.

Turning to her wardrobe, she slid on a pair of crimson T-strap heels and buckled them around her ankles. She took a few steps through the room, admiring herself in front of the mirror. Her step was light, and her feet made no sound on the floorboards. Not that anyone would be able to hear her through the laughter drifting upstairs.

Zora remembered the night her mother gave them to her.

Then, the street noises had pushed through the window of her small bedroom in their Harlem brownstone: the blaring of taxi horns, the fussing of men rolling dice and wishing for better fortunes, the trickle of jazz refrains from nearby speakeasies, the sounds of working men and women dragging their tired bodies up staircases.

Her mama's light brown hands, wrinkled and dry from scouring pans and washing vegetables, had lifted a fragile satin covering in the deepest of reds to reveal a pair of the most beautiful slippers Zora had ever seen. Even better than those that sat in the windows of shops she was never allowed into.

"I got these from Oma." Heirlooms passed down to the women in her family.

Tears had lingered in her mother's voice, her words gravelly and muffled. The mention of her mother always sent her into a deep well of sadness. "They may change."

"Change how?" Zora had asked.

"Watch and see." Her mother untied Zora's shoes and pulled them off, along with her socks. She slid the delicate slippers onto her bare feet. "They should adjust. They did for me, but I haven't worn them since she died. They'll let you come and go places without so much as a footprint left behind."

As Zora watched, the soles warmed as if she'd been curled up in front of their living room fireplace with her feet near the hearth. The backs lifted from the floor, exposing tiny new heels. Zora gasped. The ribbons transformed into a T-strap that curled around her ankle and sprouted a small golden clasp.

"No footprints?" Zora had sat forward on the bed.

"Not a single trace of you. It'll be as if you aren't even there. When you secure them tight"—her mother fastened the hook—"you will remain unheard."

"They're beautiful," Zora said as she fastened the straps. "But why are you giving them to me now?"

"You need to remain unseen until this whole thing goes away. I don't know how long that will take—weeks, months, maybe even a year or two. I will hide you for as long as it takes for folks to forget and make up stories about why that woman died. Enough time for the stories to spin on themselves." Her thick eyebrows furrowed, and sadness left lines across her forehead. "I feel like this is my fault." A single tear skated down her cheek; a deep blush set beneath the milky brown. "The magic in our blood is complicated...."

Zora caught the tear with her thumb. "No, Mama, it's my fault. My anger got the best of me. I am so very sorry. I just couldn't—"

Her mother shushed her. A knock had rattled the door. "Baby girl, it's time." Her papa's warm voice eased in.

Mama had kissed Zora's forehead, slipped the heels off, and repacked them. "Keep these close. Use them when you need to. Everything will settle again soon. The whole world is a bone knocked out of place. God'll make it right."

They were the last things her mother had packed in her suitcase.

Now Zora eased into the hallway and down the back staircase, the one that led to the kitchen, knowing her steps would be silent. Mabel leaned over a hot stove, dropping dollops of dough into oil to make fluffy beignets. With two quick leaps, Zora opened the back door.

"Who's there?" Mabel spun around, fear consuming her deep brown face.

Zora blew a kiss at her from the window, and Mabel waved. She'd always kept Zora's secrets. So far. Sometimes Zora wore the heels and sneaked up behind Mabel to have a look at what she was cooking for dinner. Mabel would get all flustered and chase her out of the kitchen with a broom. Or Zora would sneak into her shared bedroom and tug one of Ana's long corkscrew curls while she was primping and complaining about having to lend things to Zora. She loved hearing her cousin scream, then run around like a startled chicken after realizing Zora was right there.

Her T-straps left a melody only she could hear. As Zora darted out into the sticky night, Mabel threw salt over her shoulder and slammed the door.

3

*Z*ora held her breath and tried not to break into a run. Her aunt lived far enough from trouble, but close enough to find it if you were looking for it. Some called the area the back-a-town and crinkled their noses when she mentioned her street. She'd seen that flicker of judgment and shrugged it off because places where there were black and brown bodies, snippets of music, and streets laced with laughter and the scent of spicy food cooking would always be a version of home.

She took the long route so she could walk past as many houses as possible, loving how the Easter egg–colored buildings sat like old men lined up next to each other, leaning a little to the left or right, full of laughter and stories. She could pass a club where, even standing on the sidewalk, she could catch the sound of horns from famous musicians, raining down from a rooftop garden or trickling out from big open windows.

She wished she could stand here forever. But tonight, she would make music of her own.

After her aunt had forbidden her to play piano, she'd begun sneaking out. Asking her to stay away from music was like asking her to stop breathing. She started going to all the colored clubs and venues, surrounding herself with the lively chords, feeling the rattle of the rhythms prickle her skin. Then she'd found this place and charmed the owners with her voice, suggesting that she would bring the club money if they were to give her a biweekly show. Just as her mama had written—music would be her lifeline out of the mess she'd created. If anything would help the world make sense again and keep her calm, it was brass, percussion, and lilting melodies.

She tried her best not to think of them too much; each flickering memory reopened the cut. She missed her mama's round brown face. She missed going with her papa to his weekend jazz gigs to watch as he played his horn until the sun rose. This new version of her life required erasing the old. That's what Mama told her to do. Forget for a while. Be someone else until it was safe to be herself again. But it was so hard.

She shifted her satchel from her left shoulder to her right and leapt over a puddle. She turned left down North Rampart Street, brushing past two women headed home with armfuls of bags.

"Did you feel that, Geraldine?" one complained, dropping one of her bags and looking around. "Chill went straight through me." She spun around and faced Zora. "How'd you get there, girl?"

"I'm sorry," Zora replied. "I thought you saw me." She tried to hide the lie behind a smile.

"You living—or dead? There's so many darn ghosts in this town," the other replied.

"I am here in the flesh. My apologies."

"Next year, I'm going north. Gonna settle in Chicago with my son. Bet it's too cold for the spirits to linger up there. All that wind and snow will send them right on to the light or off to the devil."

Zora chuckled and turned left. "Have a good night."

Five more blocks and she'd be at the Petit Sapphire Saloon. The people in her aunt's neighborhood said that small hole-in-the-wall spot was where jazz itself was born. She didn't know if it was just something people said, stretching lies like beignet dough ready for frying, or if it was the truth. Either way, it'd become her favorite spot. The only place that made her feel a little less homesick. Her refuge since her aunt had forbidden her from playing music in the house.

She sniffed the air, filling her nostrils with the scent of rain and sulfur and heat, the scent of New Orleans. Her mama would've loved untangling the scents, for her keen nose could unravel the smells of a city or town or even house into the thousands of odors that formed the invisible stew of that place and those who inhabited it. A chef identifying ingredients. And tonight, it was the tapering storm and the pungency of crayfish and gumbos in every restaurant kitchen, the sourness of liquor, the metallic brass of the instruments, and the salt of humidity and hurricanes. They were so different from the scents that made up New York City, but she was getting used to them.

The blast of a trombone echoed, pulling her forward and leading the way. It was too hot to run, but she wanted to. She couldn't wait to cross that threshold. The club's sign hung just ahead, flanked by black gas lamps dusting the decadent clothes of well-dressed Black men and women with light. They pressed thin cigarettes and fat cigars to their mouths, taking puffs between loud peals of laughter and craning their necks to have a look inside the windows.

"Hey, little Z." Big Teddy sat at the entrance, collecting cash and tickets. His face was as round as his body, and tonight he wore a tan summer suit that matched the color of his skin. He obsessively cracked his knuckles, sending a message—he stayed ready to lump up anyone who stepped out of line.

A chorus of greetings cut through the music:

"Hey, good-looking."

"Mighty fine tonight, Zora."

"Can't wait to hear what Sweet Willow has for us this evening."

The Black Bottoms had just started their set. She'd be on next.

"Where's Jo?" she asked one of the passing servers.

"Just went in the back to get ready." The young woman pointed.

Zora zigzagged through tables of guests thumping their feet and singing along. Smiles consumed their faces, and she could feel their happiness like a cloak draped over her, making her excited to take the stage.

She darted past the kitchen through a labyrinth of offices, back into the tiny dressing room where Josephine "Jo" Robichaux had her face pressed up close to a mirror and was painting her lips bright crimson. The contrast with her light brown skin made it resemble blood.

Jo was the first friend Zora had made since arriving in New Orleans, and Zora couldn't believe she'd lasted all her eighteen years without her infectious laugh, wild taste for adventure, and deep well of kindness. She also had a voice that might rival Zora's own. Zora didn't have any siblings, but she'd love to call Jo hers. Instead, she'd heard Jo sing backup for the other bands and convinced her to sing with her, too.

"You don't need lipstick," Zora said, sneaking up on her.

Jo tsked. "Easy for you to say. Your mouth is perfectly pink. And heart-shaped! Always looking like a smudge of peanut butter with a spot of raspberry."

"You look beautiful—as always." Zora helped Jo fuss with the waves of her bob, making sure her wild frizzy curls stayed put. The humidity and heat of the room had left a sticky sheen across her neck.

Jo scoffed. "My cheeks are too red. I was out running errands with Maman without my parasol. I need to apply more powder, but I'm almost out." Zora never asked questions about where Jo came from or what her mama did for a living, because the first time she'd brought up the neighborhood to her aunt and cousins, they balked and said only bad things happened there and bad women serviced bad men.

"The problems with being passé-blanc," Zora teased.

Jo plucked her arm. "What are we singing tonight?"

"I gave the band 'A Web of Blues' last month. It's been in my head for weeks."

She hummed its refrain. "That?"

"Yes."

Jo winked. "One day you and I will be touring the world, singing our own songs. Running through the jazz clubs of Paris, too. That's where I really want to go." She rambled on about all the things she wanted to do, escaping the South to see the world. She painted the most beautiful portrait in Zora's mind.

Zora smiled at Jo's big dreams.

"Your dress is in the closet. I added another line of beads to the neck," Jo said.

Zora kissed her too-warm cheek before grabbing the beautiful garment and shimmying into it.

"Your aunt makes better ones, but I got this from Rubenstein's mail-order catalog with Maman's coupon. Figured we could share it."

Zora admired her frame in the mirror. The peacock-blue drop waist hugged her curves. She would have to borrow a step-in from her aunt's dressmaking room. Those loose undergarments would flatten her out like the women in newspapers and magazines. Her figure was identical to Jo's—and Mama's. Curves and softness. It made her miss watching her mother dress up to go dancing with her papa at the Cotton Club. "I don't want to ask her for anything. Too many questions."

"Whatever you say, Sweet Willow, who don't have a grain of sugar in her. All salt—and cayenne."

Zora laughed deeply for the first time in a long while, the kind of laugh that escapes from beneath your belly unexpectedly. She smiled and looked up at the poster on the dressing room wall advertising a portrait of her face, stage name, and a willow symbol Oma used to knit into blankets and shawls.

"Don't be shy tonight," Zora reminded her.

"I'm not shy," Jo countered.

"When the lights hit you last week, you shut like a clam. Held back your real voice."

"That old white man was there. The one that owns the Orleans Roof Garden. It used to be my favorite place to sneak into until he bought it. He makes me feel strange. Kept waving at me and ogling me with his bug eyes." Jo shuddered.

"Well, you are pretty. It's hard not to see you."

Jo Robichaux was the type of young woman you couldn't miss. When she walked into a room, her skin glowed as if she were the first sunray pressing through a window on a cold morning.

Jo hissed at Zora.

"If I see him, I'll tell Big Teddy to keep an eye out," Zora promised.

"You're the best," Jo said. She left a red lipstick kiss on Zora's cheek. "Ready?"

"Always."

A knocked rattled the door. "Y'all decent?" the club manager, Miles, shouted.

"Yes," Zora said.

Miles peered inside, his bald brown head covered in sweat. "We've got a problem."

Zora and Jo stood beside the stage. The piano player, Red, had his face perched over a bucket of vomit. His light brown cheeks held a blush almost the color of his burnt-copper hair. "I'm sorry, loves. These oysters caught me." His words sputtered out between hurls of liquid. "They got my stomach a mess."

Panic zipped through Zora. The Black Bottoms had already left the stage and packed up their things during the set break.

"We can't play without you," Jo complained. She crossed her arms and marched over to one of the Black Bottoms' brass players, ready to interrogate them as to whether they had any skill with the piano.

Zora's eyes cut to the beautiful instrument, the glow of candlelight making its cover glisten like onyx. She could play it, of course, but after what had happened with her aunt's piano, it was the one instrument she'd been avoiding. Didn't want to risk tempting the magic. She'd stick to her tiny horn and her songbird voice.

"No piano, no show. That's what everybody loves the most. We gotta cancel, baby girl." Miles put a warm hand on Zora's shoulder and looked over at the Black Bottoms, already knocking them back. "Ray has had one too many. He can't help."

"Let me think for a minute," Zora replied. "Buy me some time."

"You got it, sweetness." Miles darted off to deal with a rowdy customer at the bar.

A pair of white men approached Jo. The only white people in the club tonight. Zora immediately bristled. The color lines were as sharp as in New York, maybe sharper—and Zora's oma had been the only white person who didn't send an instant ripple of fear through her. All the people from white to light brown to black and the colors in between had different privileges and histories in this swampy city. But Black folks here still clung together like honeybees, and white folks didn't want them lingering too long in a garden they thought belonged only to them.

They made trouble even in colored spaces. Trouble nobody wanted tonight.

But Jo didn't seem worried. Her friendliness with them was puzzling and curious. Who were they? And why were they talking to Jo?

One of them turned to face her. He held a straw boater hat and stared at her with bright blue eyes. A red sunburn stripe skated down his thin nose.

He looked familiar. But from where?

The other man looked at Jo with a greasy grin. His hair was black and shaggy. Zora thought he looked like a street dog in need of a bath.

Jo waved her over. Zora shook her head. As Jo brought them closer, Zora's stomach tightened. She'd had enough of talking to strangers this evening. She didn't need to add white ones to the list.

"What are you doing?" Zora whispered to her. She tried her best to hide the prickle of fear climbing over her skin.

"Want you to meet my new friend." Jo flashed Zora a wide grin that Zora had learned meant trouble. "He brings deliveries for the clubs."

Zora knew *deliveries* meant bootlegged alcohol. The one with the greasy smile stepped forward.

"I don't want to meet new friends," Zora said to Jo. "I want to find a piano player so we can have our set. It's a packed house."

"Zora, this is Rocco Lucchese, and this is Phillip Deveraux," Jo said, ignoring Zora's desires. "Phillip's been dying to meet you."

"Dying, huh?" Zora shifted away from the one with the hat—Phillip—trying to figure out why he looked familiar. She pulled Jo to the side and whispered, "What are they doing here?" White folks usually came for shows, sat in their special section behind a red velvet rope, and left before the colored performers could exit the stage. They'd soak up all the Black music but couldn't bear to actually be close to the people who'd made it.

"Ever since you sang 'Blues for Tremé' last week, I've been waiting to say hello," Phillip interjected. "Growing up here, I've heard a lot of horn players. I thought my heart was going to stop when you played that trumpet solo. The lip trill was like nothing I've ever heard."

"Hmm . . ." Zora's eyes combed his face. It was a nice shape, and the cleft in his chin made her want to press her finger in it. Perhaps she'd seen him in the audience of her show last week, but she was now pretty confident he was also the one outside her aunt's house earlier that day. White men didn't just traipse through her colored neighborhood. "I think I've seen you before. Who are you?" Her eyes narrowed.

His eyebrows lifted, and he grinned. The candlelight exaggerated the pink of his skin. He had the tiniest gap between his teeth, which made him seem clever, and a constellation of freckles covered him. She thought he could be handsome without the sunburn. Maybe.

But Miles raced back over before she could finish. "What do you want to do? We need you onstage in about fifteen minutes. Or we've gotta call it and let everyone know. I guess I can give a free round to everyone."

"What's the problem?" Phillip asked.

"Piano player got sick on oysters," Jo blurted out. "We can't go on tonight."

Zora scowled at her for telling their business.

"I play piano," Phillip said with a big grin. One that was sort of nice, if Zora was in an admitting mood.

"No, absolutely not." Zora shook her head. Mixed bands weren't popular or allowed. The law forbade it.

"You don't trust me?"

Zora scoffed. "What do you know about colored music?"

He smiled impossibly wide at her again, and she thought that he was probably used to people always saying yes to that smile.

"We don't need help," she told him.

"Yes, we do," Jo piped up.

"We also don't need a citation for breaking the *law*. Miles especially. The police officers always come in around midnight."

"Let me worry about that," he replied with a cocky wink. "It's an emergency. I'm charming. I can handle them."

"Well, how good are your licks?" Zora shot back. "Last time you went through your octaves? Probably don't know anything about jazz."

Phillip set down his hat, his blond hair run through with a little sweat, and climbed onto the stage. He sat in front of the piano, and his fingers raced against the keys. The melody of "Ol' Man River" poured out sharp and sweet, the vibration of each note racing across her skin, almost as if he were touching her.

The club burst into applause as soon as he was done. A deep flush filled Zora as his eyes found her.

"That white boy can play."

"Got a little soul."

"Wouldn't think he had that in him. Go ahead, now."

Zora tried to push away the surprise.

"Good enough?" he called out.

"Maybe." Her mouth betrayed her as it broke into a smile.

Z ora felt at home on the stage, the lights a warm halo around her, creating a bubble that she could fill with song. The run-down glass of a chandelier even dusted everyone with beautiful tear-drops of light. She'd look out on the low tables stuffed with candles and drinks and avid listeners, and they'd become her adoring and loyal fans, showing up weekly to hear her latest song.

Her mama said she'd been born singing, calling out like an angry lark wanting to be in her own tree seven years before America entered the Great War. In fact, Oma had delivered her at home in case the magic showed up—and she'd been right to. Zora hiccuped music notes as if to charm milk and cuddles out of anyone with every hum and yelp.

Now, each time she'd stepped up here since arriving in New Orleans, the stage transported her to another place—one without the accident, without the worry, without the fear of what was next.

Phillip played the soft melody. If music notes could pour out of his fingers like they did hers, she thought, his would be the burnt oranges and butter yellows of the dawn, a sound you'd want to wake up to every morning, a song you'd never want to forget, a rhythm you'd want to slip and slide across your skin and be the refrain caught in your heart.

The beauty of it surprised her.

Her trumpet sat on a low table beside her tall microphone. She put it to her lips. She closed her eyes, imagining thousands of music strands collecting around her.

She let them out.

Jo's voice trickled beneath hers and felt like the warmest hug. If Jo could release her own notes, they'd be the color of her lipstick, wild and red and full of bravado, their melody staccato and ready for adventure.

But Phillip's music made her want to play with him forever. It sparked so many questions inside her: *How did he know how to play like this? Where did he learn?* It astonished her, the urge to let it all loose and fill the small room with a storm of music notes. Zora balled her hands into fists, careful not to let the tiny music notes completely out. She sang the last lyric, eyes closed, and the crowd burst with applause.

The set had passed too quickly, the twelve songs earning a whirlwind of claps and whistles and foot-stomping from the audience. She let the excited rumble rush over her, and only then did she open her eyes. Jo hugged her from behind, clammy arms wrapping around her torso. She thought her heart might never slow, its beat still holding the rhythm of the song they just finished. For the tiniest moment, the smallest second, she'd forgotten what she'd done and how she'd gotten here.

Jo and Zora left the stage and headed to the table where they always sat. As usual, they were brought the nightly special and a round of drinks. When Phillip followed, she was startled. Even though they'd just spent the last two hours singing and making music together, usually white folks came for shows and sat in *their* special section. Even performers would make sure they went their separate ways. The terror of police trouble settled in her stomach.

"You're going to sit here?" Zora asked.

"You'd rather me sit on the floor? Or . . ." Phillip said, slipping into the seat beside her as if he'd sat there a million times.

Jo laughed, then whispered in Zora's ear. "It'll be fine."

But Zora found that hard to believe.

"How'd I do?"

"Pretty good," Zora replied, but the word *extraordinary* whispered inside her.

"That all?" he challenged.

"Brag on yourself, much?" Her eyebrows lifted, and she cut her eyes to Jo and Rocco. They had fallen into their own bubble of conversation, which consisted of Rocco telling Jo how beautiful she was every five minutes while Jo launched into self-deprecating denials.

"So, Zora, who taught you to play like that?" Phillip pressed.

"My dad," she let slip, regretting her sudden honesty. But she didn't know how to erase him or act as if he never existed.

"Oh, he must be proud."

"He's dead," she lied, the heat of the pinch a painful flush. It was the first time she'd said the lie out loud. It made her breath catch in her throat.

"My parents are still alive, but it might as well be as if they weren't. They're almost sort of not there . . . if you know what I mean."

"Veiled." She knew much more about that feeling than she cared to admit.

"Exactly," he replied. "That's the perfect word."

They stared at each other for a long moment. She had so many questions about him; her curiosity was piqued.

Phillip started to list out all the music he'd been listening to lately, running through the famous musicians that Zora's father always loved to catch when they came through New York. She tried to keep a scowl on her face, but she couldn't stop diving into the conversation about them.

"I once saw Tell Green riff for a full fifteen minutes during 'Can't Get By.'"

Zora leaned in. "I love that song."

"Me too. He added a rest right before the chorus—made the whole room pause. It gave this extra meaning to it, you know?"

"Sort of like the rest you slipped into 'Moonlight' tonight?"

"Ah." Phillip ducked his head sheepishly. "You noticed that?"

She bit back a grin. "How could you not?" She wasn't about to admit it, but Phillip's instincts had made that song better, too. Besides her father, she'd never known someone who seemed to understand music so naturally, as though he was made up of bass lines and chords instead of muscle and bone.

A waitress set four drinks on the table. "On Big Teddy! Said you had a fantastic set. I missed it. Got stuck back in the kitchen dealing with overboiled crawfish."

Zora smiled and craned behind her to blow a kiss to the big man at the door.

Big Teddy held up his glass and whistled, causing everyone to immediately silence. "To Sweet Willow. My favorite songbird. Salut, chérie!"

As she turned back, she caught a familiar face in the crowd.

Her heart dropped.

It was Christophe Bechet Jr. from her aunt's dinner. Heat flashed inside her. He was the last person she wanted to see. If he saw she was here, he might tell her aunt, and the only good thing she had here would be gone before it really began.

Christophe started to make his way through the crowd, headed in her direction. She chugged her drink and stood.

"We've got to leave, Jo."

Jo peered up with a pout. "But I'm starving. We still need to eat," she said. "And you promised to walk me home."

Zora's stomach growled at the thought of food, but if she didn't get out of the club before Christophe reached them, she'd have more to worry about than just hunger.

"I can't—" She turned to race back to the dressing room and found Christophe a few feet away. Their eyes met. She saw his mouth start to move.

"Hey…"

Zora lost control. The magic flared, and the chandelier went out with a loud pop. The pool of darkness sent everyone scattering.

"Let's go! Let's go!" Rocco rushed them all from the table.

"What's going on?" someone shouted.

"The police," someone screamed.

They scrambled with the crowd out onto the street.

Zora didn't stop running until she was several blocks away from the Petit Sapphire. She was out of breath, her heart thudding fast, and Jo shouted out her name a hundred times.

A warm hand found her shoulder. "You all right?"

It was Phillip. His bright blue eyes searched hers. Warm, concerned.

"I'm fine," she said, taking a step back so that his arm fell. Her eyes found Rocco and Jo. They were down the street, boxed in by a late-night parade. Zora let its music flow into her until her heart found its rhythm again.

"You're not from here, are you?" Phillip asked.

"How did you know?" Zora said.

"When you grow up here, seen one, seen them all," Phillip said, cocking his head at the parade. "They lose their charm quickly."

How could anyone hate something so miraculous? she thought but didn't say. Maybe she shouldn't be so wide-eyed about it, though.

"It's the music. Reminds me of home," she said, and felt like she'd said too much.

"Where's home?" Phillip asked.

"Nowhere."

She quickly changed the subject. "How'd you learn to play the piano like that?"

"Like what, girl from nowhere?" he poked.

She tried to hide a laugh. "Didn't think you had all of that in you."

Jo and Rocco waved at them to come over. Phillip walked by her side, the peach fuzz on his arms brushing against hers, their fingers almost touching. The warmth of him hotter than the swampy evening.

"The woman who raised me—Miss Agnes—taught me about good music and how to play."

Zora knew he meant a Black housekeeper. All the rich white people around here were raised by Black nannies. Zora nodded, trying not to be annoyed with him for the way things were—Black women raised generations of white children. She imagined a Black woman sitting beside him at the piano, showing a tiny version of him how to press each white and black key.

"Her husband played with the greats—Louis Armstrong, Jelly Roll Morton, King Oliver, and more—and she had the voice of a nightingale. Should've probably been headlining her own show somewhere. Instead of helping my maman stay out of the sanatoriums my whole life."

A pinch of sadness threaded through her. "I'm sorry—I didn't mean to—"

"We've got a spell of bad luck is all. That's the way my father puts it," he said with a shrug. "And he is no good with children. That's really why I love the music so much. It was the one thing that was always there. I could count on it. Something that no bad luck, nothing terrible could touch."

Zora understood. "I know what it's like to feel that way."

"I don't believe it. Couldn't imagine you having any bad luck."

She swept past his words. "You don't know much."

"But I want to know things about you." Phillip looked at her with plain curiosity as they turned a corner. Café du Monde's bright lantern lights washed the cobblestones beneath their feet in golds. Green-and-white striped awnings stretched overhead. The full patio held hundreds of people biting into fluffy pillows of dough drenched with powdered sugar and sipping rich milky coffee.

Jo and Rocco stood there. Dozens of eyes found their spot on the sidewalk, and Jo had already pulled back. "What are you doing, Rocco?" Jo asked. "You know we can't go in there." Both Zora's and Jo's eyes found the "No Colored People and Dogs" sign—bright, clear, and bold with its rules.

"C'mon, c'mon. It's late enough." Rocco pulled Jo forward. "I know one of the servers."

"Colored people can't eat in the dining room, you know that," Zora snapped. "We have to go to the window." The words felt bitter on her tongue. She should've just gone home after their set. She should've trusted her gut. Bad things happened when she didn't listen to her instincts. Or maybe they happened when she did.

"You can hardly tell." Rocco tried to nuzzle Jo's neck.

"But that doesn't mean that I'm not colored," Jo said, upset tucking itself into her voice.

"They don't like Italians either," he pressed.

"Rocco, take it easy. Jo is right." Phillip put a hand on his shoulder, trying to calm him. But Rocco's drunken antics drew more and more attention.

Zora yanked Jo away from Rocco. "This was a bad idea."

Phillip's face flushed, and sadness filled his eyes. "I'm so sorry... for him. For everything." He reached for Zora's hand and, surprising herself, she let him take it. "Truly."

The hateful stares of white café-goers found them. Zora's stomach twisted, a knot coiling in on itself. An employee of Café du Monde marched out. "Y'all need to get. If you want something, you know the rules." His blue gaze burned as it landed on Zora and Jo, the reminder a hot slap.

"Don't talk to them that way," Rocco threatened. "Do you know who I work for?"

Phillip put a hand on Rocco's chest and held him back before turning to the employee. "He's drunk. He doesn't mean any harm. We don't want any trouble."

Zora quickly took Jo's arm and walked away. They didn't speak, the anger a ribbon between them. They were used to not being able to go certain places but not to making a spectacle out of it. Zora could see Jo fighting tears of embarrassment.

"I can give you a ride." Phillip chased behind them. "I'm parked close." He pointed at a gaudy red car. It looked like a Popsicle.

Rocco's voice was sloppy with drink. "It's a Chrysler Imperial Eighty. The car everybody in the great state of Louisiana wishes they had."

Zora rolled her eyes. Her mama always said if you had to stand on your money and not your heart, then you were of poor spirit. But as Rocco leered at his reflection on the red hood, Phillip was looking at the car with a quiet pride. "It's the first thing I've bought with my own money, my way. I wanted something that could help me escape home, even if just for a little while ... with a pretty song in a nightclub." He turned to her. "Offer still stands. I could drop you and Jo off."

Zora saw that a police car had pulled up to the corner. The Café du Monde employee rushed over to the window. More curious eyes found them, and the magic inside her welled up once more, collecting in an angry storm. She was afraid she'd burst at any moment.

Zora shook her head. "We should go."

She and Jo walked off quickly into the sticky night. She let herself look back at the boy with the sunburn and the kind eyes, with hands that played the piano like she'd never heard. If only there was a world in which she could have taken that ride. That is, if she were interested in white boys ... or any boys, really ... which she most certainly was not.

5

The next week, Zora sat her annoyance on her elbow and stared out the streetcar window.

Her cousins were arguing about whom Christophe Bechet Jr., the one they voted as the best looking from last week's dinner, would be courting. He was supposed to come for tea with his mother later that day, and the sound of his name put her on edge, wondering if this afternoon would be when he'd volunteer her secret, ruining the only spot of happiness she'd managed to get for herself here. Somehow, though, her cousins' bickering made her more exasperated than anything else at the moment.

Ana and Evelyn started tugging the note from Christophe's mother between them.

"Give it to me. I want to see it," Ana demanded.

"No, when Christophe Jr. dropped it off, he handed it to *me*." Evelyn pressed it to her chest.

"That doesn't mean you own it—and get to hog it." Ana reached to snatch it. "The address says to all the women in the Broussard household. That means me, too."

They fussed over the invitation, almost ripping it in half. Aunt Celine flicked her red-polished nails against the screen that separated white passengers from colored ones.

The streetcar slugged down Canal Street. The mid-August heat was like an oppressive rider with a terrible body odor. Outside, rich white men and women strolled about, parasols protecting them from the sun as they waved ornate fans to cool their pink faces. "On our way back, we'll get a black-star one," Aunt Celine said, sucking her teeth. "It was too hot to wait today, but I don't like sitting back here like luggage. I'd rather be in the colored trolley." Zora knew that when her aunt wasn't traveling with her browner daughters—or even her— she would pass for white in order to be treated nicely, fooling folks into thinking she'd come from off the boats in the port, from Spain or

Italy like many of the others in this city. Her mama had done it, too, back home when necessary.

Usually, Zora loved riding the streetcars, but today she would rather have been reading sheet music and preparing for her next show at the Petit Sapphire . . . and, if she was in an admitting mood, seeing Phillip again and talking to him about music. Aside from Jo, it'd been so long since she had someone to talk to about the thing she loved the most. Jo mostly wanted to sing, never indulging all of Zora's desires to dive into musical theory or discuss the mechanics of different instruments or uncover all the history of music in the city or study sheet music. She'd wave her away with a delicate flick of her hand or start singing to stamp out all of Zora's thousands of thoughts and feelings and questions until Zora would sing along with her. But what Zora coveted the most was being enveloped in it all.

"You have bags under your eyes, girl," Aunt Celine said to her. "I must teach you to take more pride in your appearance."

She'd only slept a few hours. Nightmares kept her up listening to a late-night storm, and now she was being forced to go look at stupid dresses for the season. A practical person, she only needed a few to wear during the day and a pretty one or two for her performances. But Aunt Celine felt differently.

"Being a debutante will require that. It's an art form, you know," Aunt Celine had said.

The streetcar motion and the heat began to tug her to sleep.

She was back in a dream version of New York City with her mama, inching up the rickety service elevator to the penthouse of oil tycoon Mrs. Abigail Marie Abernathy, her mama's most loyal and demanding client.

Her own words to Mama haunted her: "Chef, what's for dinner?"

Her mama had beamed so large, Zora could almost count all her teeth. "Roasted duck stuffed with foie gras and bacon-wrapped asparagus, then maybe eggplant, and a chess pie for dessert." The way she spoke about food was the way Zora and Papa spoke about music; instruments were their medium, and food was Mama's. "Maybe even a hummingbird cake, too. People love options, especially sweet ones."

The elevator's door slid open, depositing them in the penthouse's mudroom before creaking off. Mrs. Abernathy stood with her thin white arms crisscrossed over her chest and a deep red in her cheeks that wasn't from blush. "You get in here right now. I don't pay you to be nice to the staff. I hear you spend more time cozying up with them than in here with me." She yanked Mama's arm and pulled her into the kitchen.

Zora flinched, ready to protest, but her mother shot her a look that told her to remain silent. Mama held back a grimace. Zora knew she disliked her client, but she tried her best to put on a good face.

A hand pulled on Zora's shoulder, wrenching her from the dream. For a moment, it felt like Mrs. Abernathy's hand.

Aunt Celine was staring at her, irritated. "You're screaming," she hissed. "What's wrong with you?"

All the other passengers, both colored and white, gawked in her direction. Her cheeks warmed with embarrassment. She was not supposed to be drawing attention to herself. Yet her own dreams were betraying her.

Zora wiped her eyes. "I didn't sleep well yesterday."

"She's always like this at night," Ana reported. "That's why we *hate* sharing our room with her. We get woken up at least once with all her *racket*."

Evelyn snickered behind her paisley fan.

Zora wanted to counter with how loudly they both snored, but she was still embarrassed. She apologized again instead and resumed looking out the window.

"Don't worry, girls. I have just the thing to fix her."

Zora didn't know what her aunt had in mind. Maybe locking her away in the attic. Maybe having those church ladies come back to the house to pray over her again. Maybe forcing her to take more of those vitamins she claimed purified the soul.

The streetcar lurched to a stop.

"We're getting off here. Thank God," her aunt said.

They trundled down the streetcar's staircase and stood at the bustling corner of Canal Street and Dauphine Street, where the store Maison Blanche stretched high above them.

"Put your gloves on, girls. I only need a short while, then we'll be on our way."

Even though it was close to ninety degrees outside, each one of them slipped on their dainty lace gloves. Zora ran her fingers along her initials sewn into the palms until her heart slowed and the tension left her muscles. The letter Z almost looked like an S. They were the one thing that her aunt had made for her after lecturing her about lacy patterns making a lady's fingers look elegant and dainty. They'd quickly become her favorite.

Her aunt wrestled a tiny sketchbook from her purse and placed a pencil in her bun. She took a deep breath, stretched her neck high, and strode inside. Zora felt like one of three little ducklings as she and her cousins trailed her aunt in a line.

The high ceiling was adorned with massive chandeliers that dusted all the wonders with light. Tiny alcoves held all manner of dresses: cotton ones for tea and daywear and dropped-waist ones of satin and tulle and beads for evening and dancing. Glass counters contained twinkling jewelry. Hatboxes sat in perilous towers. Perfume scented the hot, muggy air.

All of the white attendants swiveled around. One strode up angrily. "Excuse me! Excuse me!"

Zora held her breath. Even in New York City, she and her mama knew which stores to visit so they'd be allowed in and not hassled.

She wondered if life would always be this way. Colored folks needing to bend themselves into shapes to deal with white people, needing to soften their tongues or adopt different personalities. Would they ever be allowed to go into stores and restaurants? Would they ever get the chance to spend their hard-earned money like everyone else? Would they ever be welcome?

"You know you can't—" the woman started.

"Yes, we know we can't try on the dresses," her aunt replied with the softest voice Zora had ever heard her use.

"Or touch them," the woman reminded. "You can place orders from the catalog."

Aunt Celine held up a gloved hand, flashing the beautiful lace. "Sometimes I like to see how things hang before ordering."

The white woman examined them, her green eyes taking in their pretty dresses and perfect bobs and dainty sandals, then bit her bottom lip. "Just this once. Be quick about it. The store is mostly empty," she said, letting them pass. The heat of her stare lingered on their backs.

"How gracious of you," Aunt Celine remarked, and Zora knew she was trying not to let the snarl in her upper lip show.

Other white store clerks craned their necks to have a look at them. Ana and Evelyn wandered in and out of the sections, taking turns to block their mom from view as she made quick sketches in her book.

"Terrible beadwork. Such plain lace," her aunt grumbled. "They have the nerve to be charging ten dollars and ninety-five cents apiece."

Bored as her aunt went from one dress to another, Zora ran her fingers over the velveteen stripes on a nearby hatbox. Music poured through an open window, and she started to hum. It was one of the songs from the night she played with Phillip—"Moonlight." His face appeared in her mind. His sunburned nose, the light freckles on his skin. He would probably argue with her about the percussion, how it probably needed more bass. The thought of it made her smile unexpectedly and relax too much. Her fingers warmed, and a tiny music note slipped out, dancing along the edges of the hatbox ribbon.

"Maman, she's doing it again," Ana said, pointing at Zora.

Her bubble burst and she stopped humming. The note drifted off. Ana shoved Evelyn, determined to catch it. Evelyn pivoted, and they both crashed into a nearby mannequin.

Aunt Celine glanced up, her eyes narrowing to slits. The few white folks in the store whispered and pointed.

The clerk rushed over again. "Get out of here right now. I knew you'd be trouble."

Aunt Celine tucked her sketchbook into her bag. Zora felt queasy from the stares. Once outside in the sun, Aunt Celine whipped around. "Ana and Evelyn, I'll handle you both when I get home. You're not too old for the switch. All I asked was for a few hours of peace." She pivoted to Zora. "And *you*. I told you about all that nonsense. I told your mama and your daddy I'd have none of it. I'm calling the conjure woman."

Ana and Evelyn gasped.

"She'll take care of the evil lurking inside you. Stamp it out, that's what."

The magic in Zora's veins flared. What was a conjure woman? What did her aunt want done to her? What would her mama say?

Aunt Celine's bark could be heard through the house as she ordered Mabel around. Ana and Evelyn primped wildly, preparing for tea with Christophe Bechet Jr. and his mother. Ana and Evelyn were doing their best to terrify Zora about the conjure woman.

"Mama B's going to make you chew on roots," Ana said as she sprayed herself with a cloying rose perfume.

Zora had never seen a conjure woman, or even heard of one. Only hucksters with their crystal balls full of promises in New York City.

"I bet she'll put those rods in her ear. Lure the devil out," Evelyn added. "The conjure women here don't play around. They call their spirits."

Zora's imagination filled with horrific images of Mama B: bent at the shoulders like a broken hinge, draped in an old-fashioned frock coat too hot for this heat, with a long black dress underneath it, swishing back and forth like a church bell. She saw leathery brown skin, a face with a roadmap of experience.

"Last month she pulled a demon out of Violette DuBois by setting a flame across her skin. Burned it right out of her," Ana said.

Zora didn't know if she believed any of it. But would losing her magic be the worst thing? She ran through the reasons why it wouldn't: what happened with Mrs. Abernathy in New York, the fear of who she might become if she kept it, and the fact that she missed her parents desperately and wished she could go home.

A knock rattled the door. "Girls." Mabel's sweet voice drifted inside. "Your maman said come on down. The Bechets are arriving."

Ana and Evelyn scrambled to finish their hair and adjust their dresses. Zora tentatively followed behind, not wanting to earn another tongue-lashing from her aunt for being late. Then she paused, frozen with fear now that the moment of truth had come. Would Christophe reveal her secret?

The sitting room table had been covered in white doilies and boasted tiered platters of macarons, tiny sandwiches, and tarts. Petite porcelain teapots sat among dainty teacups and expertly polished spoons. Christophe and his mother stood beside Aunt Celine, admiring the spread.

"Girls, girls, isn't it lovely that Mrs. Bechet and Christophe have come to pay us a visit today?"

Ana giggled, and Evelyn elbowed her. Zora inched forward. Christophe wore linen pants and a collarless shirt. His skin glistened with a slight sheen of sweat, reminding Zora of almonds drizzled with honey, and he'd shaved his peach fuzz of a mustache. His eyes found hers. He smiled. The warmth of it surprised her.

"Hello, Zora," he said, his voice thick and deep. He wasn't bad looking. She could suddenly see why her cousins were so fond of him.

They settled in the puffy high-backed chairs. Aunt Celine and Mrs. Bechet launched into a pile of gossip and worries about how busy the fall would be, and how quickly Mardi Gras would be upon them, and how Aunt Celine's dress orders had started to come in for the upcoming season.

Zora found a spot outside the window. If she just behaved, she'd soon be back in the room with her cat and her journal, scribbling music refrains and planning out her next set for the Petit Sapphire. So long as Christophe didn't tell everyone about Sweet Willow.

"Daydreaming?" Christophe whispered, leaning closer.

Zora thought about ignoring him. "You could say that."

"You're very talented, you know? I wanted to tell you that—"

Zora flinched, bracing herself. She let her eyes burn into his as he squirmed in his seat.

"I'm not going to say anything," he replied, his voice low. "My maman doesn't even know that I sneak out to go to clubs. She'd tan my hide if she found out. So if you keep my secret, I'll keep yours."

A wave of relief flooded her.

"Maman doesn't approve of the music I like," Christophe whispered to Zora. "Thinks it's from the devil. Says it comes straight out of hell itself."

Zora laughed, imagining some cracks in the cobblestones and the vapors of hell releasing both steam and music.

"Also, I'm not a snitch," he added. "That's my brother, Jean-Claude."

They both laughed at that.

"Your secret is safe with me," Christophe continued.

Zora shot him a grateful look. "And yours with me."

Aunt Celine and Mrs. Bechet gazed over at them, nodding with approval. Evelyn, neglected, picked at her sandwich. Ana leaned over to Christophe and peppered him with questions. While he answered each one, he stole glances at Zora.

Mabel brought out a plate of hot beignets piled high with snowy sugar. Mrs. Bechet exclaimed with delight.

Christophe leaned forward, close to Zora's ear. "I'd love to show you more clubs if you're up for it. A bunch of new spots I think you'd like have opened up on North Rampart. I can give you a whole tour of the neighborhood."

Zora paused, looking up at her aunt's expectant face. A wave of gratitude washed over her. He hadn't told. He wasn't *going* to tell. She could keep playing. Maybe she could even find new spots to perform.

"I'd love to."

6

hree days later, Zora held an appointment card tentatively, glancing down at the licorice-black calligraphy.

The AceJack Pharmacy

435 South Rampart Street

Mama B can decode your dreams, keep the devil

away, and attend to all your magical needs.

SHATTERED MIDNIGHT

The storefront looked like it belonged in the underworld if there was such a place. A darkness settled over it despite the hot afternoon sun, and a crimson glow emanated from bulbous globes dangling in the big window. Through the glass, one could see endless shelves of containers. The storefront had been painted cream and sparkled with curlicue trim and golden accents. A tattered sign dropped from above the doorway and announced in faded cursive lettering: "The AceJack Pharmacy."

"Go on in there. We'll be waiting around the corner," Aunt Celine ordered. "Good Christian people who know the Lord don't dabble in these things. But I had no choice." She shooed Zora off the curb. Ana and Evelyn hovered behind their mother like two little girls ready to hide in her skirts.

Zora gulped and tiptoed closer. She opened the door and stepped in. "Hello," she said in a soft voice.

She'd never seen anything like it. Shelves held bottles advertising strange goods with strange promises: John the Conqueror's Great Love Compound, Lucky Mojo Magnets, Master Keys to Fortune and Happiness, Van Van Incense Powders, Ayer's Sarsaparilla Purity Pills, Fitzgerald's Brain Salt Boost, and more.

Zora quailed. She saw skulls set on ledges, and she was certain their jaws twitched. An eerie trumpet trill sounded beyond the walls and beneath the wood of the floor. The candles flickered, threatening to bathe her in darkness with all of these oddities, and she would've sworn each plant she passed hissed at her.

She'd had faint memories of Oma and Granddaddy's old pharmacy on West 137th Street and Lenox Avenue. But it was nothing like this. They'd sold home remedies and filled prescriptions for colored folks in Harlem when other places wouldn't. The counters were just high enough for her little-girl fingers to reach.

"Your soul is heavy," a voice snapped from behind.

Zora jumped. The woman rocked back and forth on her heels. Zora tried not to gasp.

First of all, she was impossibly beautiful—nothing like the hag Zora had pictured. She wasn't in black. Her skin was the perfect shade of brown, like freshly made pralines, and she had a pink bow of a mouth. Though they were inside, a large plum hat crested over her black curls, and she wore a dress that reminded Zora of a sweet French tart.

Zora had seen so many strangers drift in and out of New York City, a tide of restless bodies creating the pulse of that grand place. But she'd never seen a person like this before.

"Didn't mean to frighten you, but this ain't a place for little chickens. It's a place where real work is done. Decisions are made and consequences administered," the woman said, her voice a tinkling melody of terror. "I'm Bernadette Beauvoir, but everyone calls me Mama B."

"S—I mean—Zora Broussard."

Her mouth twitched. "That's what you answer to, eh?"

Mama B's gaze passed through her, down into her heart, and its trail burned. Zora had not known that one person could be this terrifying. She looked back at the door, wishing she could see her aunt's back from her spot. "What is this place?"

"A pharmacy, of course."

"Never ever seen one like this."

"You ain't seen much, then, girl." She clucked her tongue. "It's a laboratory of magic, if you want to get technical." Mama B stared at her, hard. "Magic leaves a trace, and you stink of it. You've got two threads coursing through you from both your grandmothers—the colored one and the white one. It's in your blood. All that music—all that power."

A calm suddenly washed over Zora. She didn't know if it came from the woman or from her first chance at not having to hide since New York.

"Come sit!" Mama B closed the pharmacy's front door, flipping the "Closed" sign in the window, and then bent over the room's unlit hearth. With a snap of her fingers, it went from an empty pit to one full of fire. "I can feel the trouble inside you. Spirit's unsettled."

"So you knew? Did my aunt tell you?"

"She squawked on and on about all sorts of things. But as soon as you walked in here, I could feel it. You're a tiny tornado, and she wants all of that gone." The woman's forehead crinkled with irritation as she placed herbs and flowers into the fire. White smoke left a perfume behind.

Zora swallowed and prepared to tell the truth of what she did. "It made me do something . . . caused an accident. It's why I'm here in this city to begin with. And it's just caused a mess of everything. I can't control it."

The woman waved her hands around, wafting the smoke. "There are many wielders on this earth, honey. Magic doesn't do that, the practitioner does." The woman took her hand and closed her eyes.

"New Orleans is a pocket of enchantment. There's deep-rooted magic from those who were originally on this land, and those from all corners of the world who continue to come now. Like yourself. That energy's caught in the cobblestones and the graves. In the air."

Tears welled in Zora's eyes. "She hurt my mother. But . . . but . . . I didn't mean to hurt her. I . . . I . . . just wanted Mrs. Abernathy to stop."

"You've got to say it if you want me to."

Zora realized that she'd never said it out loud. It had lived in her chest, growing thornier every day. Anxiety piled up, and she was thick with fearful guilt. "I—I want to get rid of my gifts."

"Do you know what you wish? How big that is, girl? You were very angry. Very angry. And she paid with her life. These are the rules. All of us who can pull at magic have similar wells. They just come out differently is all."

"I don't even know how to use it. Or control it."

"You're a young woman now. Those excuses don't hold any longer." Mama B squeezed her hand. Zora felt a warmth radiate from her hand as if she'd caught a falling star.

The tears Zora had tried so hard to fight rushed out of her eyes. The deep ones that she'd buried and hidden. Mama B didn't let go of her hand and didn't say a word until she'd gotten every last one out.

"If I take this magic from you, you'll feel very alone," Mama B said. "And you're already lonely."

"It's what I deserve," Zora grumbled.

"Who gets to decide that? Are you the Almighty? You the one that gave yourself those gifts?" she challenged.

"No, ma'am. But I'm the one who can't control them. I decided to hurt Mrs. Abernathy. I wanted her to pay." The admission made Zora feel lighter.

A deep silence followed.

Then: "If you want your magic gone, it's not going to be that simple." Mama B's eyebrows lifted.

Adrenaline flooded through Zora. Maybe this was her chance to live a normal life—to go home to her parents, to follow her dreams without having to hide them. "What do I have to do? I'll do whatever it takes. I promise. Anything."

"Be careful with promises. Broken ones create ripples." She inspected Zora, eyes combing over the intricacies of her face. "You've got deep magic on both sides of your family. It will take serious rooting out."

Zora blinked. Magic on *both* sides. She'd only ever known about the powers from Oma's line. She thought about her dad's family, about his beloved mother, Queenie, whom she'd never met.

It didn't matter. Neither grandmother was here to help her now.

"I want it gone," she repeated more firmly now, the declaration almost burning her skin.

"Is this what *you* really want or that aunt of yours?"

Both, she thought. *One thing we can agree on.*

Zora flashed her a tentative smile.

"Hmm, okay." Mama B went to a nearby cabinet of labeled glass containers—patchouli, lavender, jasmine, bergamot, orange blossom, and more. She put her hands in each, adding to an empty jar. Then she dropped in a metal object.

"First, you must wait until after the water comes through. Storms plague this city. Mess with magic. Too thick. I reckon the water is cursed from the Heinrich family. They brought their troubles with them."

Who was the Heinrich family? What did they have to do with it? But there were more pressing questions gnawing at her. "If I get rid of it, can I erase what happened?" All the possibilities swirled around inside her. Maybe she could make this right.

Mama B shook her head. "What you ask for is the past to be changed—for a door to be opened and what has come before to be rearranged. That means lives unlived, lives undone. Magic erased from the bloodline and unraveled."

"But—"

"You want too much, girl. You ask for everything—and nothing, not even magic, can give you that."

Zora's hopes fell.

"Now, pay attention," said Mama B. "You have to meet me in St. Louis Cemetery Number One. You hear? Come on October thirty-first right before midnight. The veil will be thinnest."

Halloween. Zora did a quick calculation. Two months away.

"The veil?" Zora thought of her mama's letter. How she'd veiled Zora in New Orleans.

Mama B shook her head. "You're building a door to the other side.

The magic must be sent there. The ancestors gave it, so the ancestors must take it back."

Zora felt cold. "How much will this cost? I . . . I . . . don't have much money. I know I can get it if you give me a little time."

"I don't need money, child. I have plenty. Enough for this lifetime. There are a lot of cheating men in this town with wives eager to keep them at home." She closed her eyes. "Magic has its own price. You must trade something you love for something you don't."

Zora waited.

"You have a pair of ruby-red shoes," Mama B said.

Zora's toes curled in her saddle shoes.

"Those are half my price."

Only half? And Zora's mama would be devastated. She was caught in a tangle of indecision. She decided to lie. She opened her mouth to say she didn't know what Mama B was talking about.

Mama B tsked, as if to cut her off before she spoke. "This kind of feat requires sacrifice."

"What's the second thing?"

"The music."

"But—but—" Her heart plummeted into her stomach.

"You cannot have one without the other," she replied simply. "And remember—the magic will only be satisfied if all parties keep their word. Do we have a deal?" She held out her hand.

Zora stared at her feet. Her pulse hammered. Sweat skated down her back. Clashing thoughts banged around in her mind. She could never stop playing music. The music was all she had. It was her life.

But what kind of life is it if you're constantly looking over your shoulder? another voice asked.

Her magic—that was dangerous, deadly. She knew that all too well. It had taken away her home, her family.

Could she let it take the music, too?

Did she have a choice?

Zora gulped, took Mama B's hand, and gave it a firm shake.

"I'll meet you in the graves near Congo Square just before midnight on October thirty-first. Don't be late. Bring the shoes. The magic in your blood grows stronger and stronger."

She handed Zora the container now filled with dried roots. On top was a skeleton key.

"What's this for?"

"A little something to ease your spirit. Put it under your bed and bring it back to me when we see each other again."

Zora clutched the glass jar to her chest and ran out of the pharmacy. With every step she took toward her aunt and cousins, she told herself that her magic would be gone and that she'd be able to fix at least one thing.

The rogue notes of a clarinet spilled onto the street, and Zora felt her heart ache.

October. That meant she only had two months before having to say goodbye to the greatest love of her life.

Zora waited to get ready for bed after her cousins' chorus of snores filled the room. She sat in the window with her cat curled up beside her and the jar that Mama B gave her resting on her lap. Rain skated down the windows as an August storm passed through, and she squinted in the subtle darkness at the tangled ingredients.

"She said this will help me sleep," Zora whispered to the cat.

He looked up at her.

"I wish you could talk to me. I wish you could tell me what to do." Zora tapped her fingers along the glass, drumming a tiny melody to blend with the rain. Music notes drifted from her fingers, the same size as the fat stormy drops. "What if I can never play an instrument again? What if I won't be able to sing?"

The cat nudged the glass lid off, and the scent of herbs and oils filled both their noses. A crash of lightning made Zora squeeze her eyes shut. The face of Mrs. Abernathy filled the darkness of her mind. The fateful night where everything went wrong played on a loop, a moving picture show stuck on repeat. The memories washed over her.

She found herself at the corner of Fifth Avenue and East Seventy-Seventh Street again, with Mama at her side as they made their way to Mrs. Abernathy's penthouse. She held Mama's favorite cast-iron skillet, the one she never cooked without.

"Why can't you just quit—like Daddy said? She's mean as a junk-yard dog."

"She tips for the trouble—and is loyal. I don't have to take many jobs because of her."

Their favorite doorman, Georgie, waited for them. Pudgy and white, he always chuckled when he saw them, big belly bounding up and down with happiness. "Evening, Mrs. Aggie, Miss Sadie. My favorite duo. Need help?" He reached out his big arms to take their parcels like always.

"I've got my right hand with me." Mama motioned at Zora with a wink. "And you're just trying to flirt your way into a piece of pound cake. I'm familiar with your antics, mister."

"I'd eat a rock if you made it, Mrs. Aggie," he'd replied, and used the phone to call for the service elevator.

"I'll be sure to have Sadie run you down some dessert once the party is in full swing," her mother had promised.

"You spoil me," he said with a grin.

Zora heard the wobbly elevator reach the main floor. She hated the way it felt to always have to enter through the back of the building and take this jumpy elevator the white rich folks stuffed with staff up and down. If one elevator was to malfunction and plummet to the basement, it'd be that one.

"I'll warn you, Mrs. Aggie, that whole apartment has been like the Great War itself." Georgie's blue gaze dropped to his feet.

"Ain't it always?" her mama had replied.

"We can hear them all the way down here. All her shouts coming through the pipes"—he leaned down and his voice dropped to a whisper—"'cause yesterday a lady showed up with a baby."

"A baby?" Zora had exclaimed.

Georgie waved his hand. "Ssshh! Rich folks are always listening and ready to fire somebody. Like they done bought a second pair of ears. Most of 'em got enough money to." He cleared his throat and looked around before imparting more of the salacious details. "Mr. Julius's other lady showed up. And that baby in her arms was just a-hollering like it knew it was born from sin."

Her mama gasped and shook her head, murmuring over and over again, "This isn't good at all. Not one little bit."

"She's been yelling at everyone. The elevator's too slow or someone's voice is too high or she wanted her packages delivered in a certain way or she wanted pink roses and not red ones, and so on, and so forth."

Zora's mouth dropped open, and Mama reached over and firmly closed it.

"Thank you for the warning, Georgie. You're one of the reasons I keep coming around here," she said. "I'll be sure to whip up something that soothes tonight. Take the edge off."

"We'd be grateful. She's had us walking on glass—not even egg-shells, ma'am—all day." He tipped his hat as the elevator doors opened, and the spindly porter stared back with haunted eyes. This white man never greeted them. Georgie said he didn't talk much, but Zora thought he just didn't like colored people, on account of the way he'd ease away if they got too close.

"See you later, Georgie," Mama called as she and Zora stepped inside the too-hot box.

SHATTERED MIDNIGHT

Mrs. Abernathy complained from the moment they arrived, pacing as they set up, the click-clack of her heels an angry melody beneath her complaints and worries.

"The food has to be the best you've ever made, Aggie. They've all been talking about me. Gossiping. And I won't be outdone."

"They have to know that I throw the best parties on the whole of Fifth Avenue."

"Give them something so delicious it'll make them forget."

"I am the most beautiful woman who throws the most beautiful parties and everyone should want to eat at my table."

Sweat poured down Mama's cheeks, a deep flush working its way through the brown. Zora had never seen her look so harassed.

"Mama, let me help."

"No, no. This has to be right, baby," she whispered as Mrs. Abernathy turned her attention to the maid who rushed in and out of the dining room with the silverware. "I just have to get her to try one of these canapés. They've got something in them that will soothe her."

Zora knew what that meant. Mama was breaking her rule. The no-magic rule.

"You can help me by going into the dining room and counting the place settings. She didn't tell me how many we were feeding tonight, and I don't want to hear her call me an idiot, claiming that she did."

"Yes, ma'am." Zora slipped into the dining room. The high-ceilinged room featured one long table. The maid, Annabella, adjusted the prettiest china Zora had ever seen and lit a series of candles that left stripes of buttery light across the lace tablecloth. She was about to ask her how many settings there were when a cry escaped the kitchen.

Her mama's.

Zora and Annabella raced back through the kitchen door and entered to a horrible scene.

Mrs. Abernathy grasped her mama, holding a candle to the underside of her arm. She could smell her mama's flesh burning. While she gripped her, Mrs. Abernathy was hurling insults. Her mama was trapped.

Zora hadn't called on her magic. She'd only felt the ferocious need to protect her mother.

Her notes catapulted out of her in an explosion. Black sheets thick as mud flipped over pots and pans and sent dishes clattering to the floor. Candles toppled and set kitchen towels and curtains ablaze. The magic toppled all the chairs and the table. The cabinets tumbled from the walls. The pantry dropped its contents.

The floor cracked and crumbled as if an earthquake had ruptured it. Mrs. Abernathy screeched. And then she fell through and down the hole.

They heard a sickening thump. And the screaming shifted—one pitch had been snuffed out, but another kept going.

Mama acted quickly, dragging Zora to the fire escape. Zora hadn't even realized *she* was screaming until her mother told her to stop. "Baby girl, you have to hold it in," she hollered.

Zora's throat was raw, and all she heard was a ringing in her ears as Mama clamped a hand over her mouth, as if she were trying to shove it all back in. Everything she'd done. All the magic.

Zora let her mother drag her down the metal staircases, down to the ground, as the building rumbled and shook. Her voice tapered off. Raw. Warbly. Broken.

"We've got to get out of here, baby," she heard Mama whisper.

They darted past taxis and fancy cars, barely making it across Fifth Avenue and into Central Park. She looked back to see people streaming out like ants from a stomped hill. Slowly, the building started to collapse inward.

Zora woke with a jolt. She saw the silhouette of a woman in a fancy church hat and the outline of another—a woman who looked like Oma.

Suddenly, the outlines evaporated, and Evelyn's scowling face greeted her. "You were having a bad dream," she said. "Could've woken up Ana—or Mama."

Zora's throat was raw, just like in the dream. She tugged her damp nightgown away from her skin. "Who were those women?" she asked.

"What women?" Evelyn's scowl grew deeper. Even the cat gazed up in curiosity. "What's in that jar?" Evelyn pointed.

"The conjure woman gave it to me for bad dreams...but I don't think it worked," Zora said, pulling her knees to her chest and rocking back and forth, trying to soothe herself. The cat licked her hand.

"Zora? This happens almost every week," Evelyn said.

Zora felt too weak not to tell her. "I did something bad back home. Something very bad."

Evelyn's eyes bulged, and she stood. Zora suddenly realized her cousin was already dressed. "We've been thinking you might have gotten with child. Been waiting for you to get sick or for you to start showing."

Zora wanted to say that being unwed and pregnant might've actually been a better fate than the one she was facing. She shook her head. "It's not that."

Ana rolled over and started talking in her sleep. They both froze. Evelyn placed a finger to her mouth. They held their breaths and waited until Ana mumbled herself back into a snore.

As she watched, Evelyn slipped over to the door. "Don't say anything, all right?" Evelyn asked. Stunned, Zora nodded once as Evelyn disappeared.

She moved to the window nook, holding the cat. Moments later, through the sheets of rain, she spotted Evelyn's parasol disappear around the corner.

Zora gaped. She never would have dreamed her cousins had a

life outside these walls. Where was Evelyn headed? What secrets did *she* have?

Zora shook her head. The heat and rattle of the dream buzzed through her, making her terrified to close her eyes again. She left the window nook. "I couldn't sleep anymore tonight if I wanted to. I'm going to head out, too," she whispered to the cat. Outside, the nightmares of Mrs. Abernathy would move on like a hurricane running out of wind.

She dressed in the dark, then gazed out into the storm right outside the window once more. Was Evelyn also doing something that could threaten all she held dear?

But she figured she might as well mind her business. She had so many secrets of her own.

Zora sat at a side table at the Petit Sapphire. Jelly Roll Morton had just started his set, and she instantly felt better. One of her favorite servers brought her a piece of fried fish and a square of corn bread. She wouldn't have to sneak back into the house for hours.

For a brief moment, she let herself think of her papa. How he'd critique Jelly Roll Morton's trumpet solo, how the piano player struck the keys a millisecond too late, how the lady singing backup slurred her words, having obviously had one too many. Would she still feel the music of others as deeply without the magic? What would Oma tell her to do?

One song after another massaged her tense nerves. She'd have about two months of this left. She wanted to soak in every single moment.

A voice broke her concentration. "You waiting for someone?"

Phillip stared down at her. He looked as intense as if he was examining a diamond, not a person.

"What are you doing here?" she asked, excitement mingling with wariness.

"Listening to ol' Jelly Roll Morton try to get through his set. Working up the nerve to come talk to someone."

"And who might that someone be?" she replied.

"Let me tell you about her," he said, taking a seat at her table. "She's this beautiful young singer. She performs here sometimes."

Zora looked around, nervous that others would see a white man sitting beside her. They'd gotten away with it once, but it didn't make her any less on edge.

"Oh, does she?" Zora's cheeks flamed.

"You wouldn't believe what she does with 'Heart Blues.'"

Zora's eyebrows lifted with surprise. She hadn't performed that song yet here. How could he . . .

"I was helping Miles about a month ago. Pulling cases through the back door. I like to do odd jobs here when I can, be close to the music. I heard it drifting through the hall. Calling me to a dressing room. I pressed my ear against it. I had to listen."

Zora's heart flickered. "That's one of my mama's favorite songs."

"I love the way you slowed down the refrain. Made it even more . . . elegiac."

She felt more heat, and the club was already sticky with it. "What's this person's name? The one you're working up the nerve to speak to?" she asked.

He grinned. "Her stage name is Sweet Willow. But she hasn't been sweet to me . . . yet."

Zora's own laugh betrayed her. "No one could be sweet in this heat." She lifted her hand fan and flapped it, grateful it could hide her smile.

"You would look beautiful even if it was a thousand degrees."

Zora eyed him, weighing the depth and sincerity of his words. Despite her suspicion, talking to a fellow musician—one, she had to admit, who made her stomach unexpectantly flip—was filling the small, lonely cracks in her new life, a place where nobody knew the real Zora. "You have a thing for colored girls or something?"

"I have a *thing* for beautiful women like yourself."

"Hmph. Probably got a girl in every parish." Zora rolled her eyes, trying to keep her mouth from smiling.

"You usually full of so many assumptions?" he asked.

"I've seen your type . . . in New York," she lied. Her mama and papa hadn't really let her see much of anything.

"Oh, so that's where you're from. Well, I hope it's a good one. Speaking of which, I'm also trying to find a way to apologize for the other night. My friend Rocco is an—"

"Ass," she interrupted.

"I won't even attempt to deny it. And there's no excuse. He knows how things are. He should've never tried to get you and Jo to enter Café du Monde. It's upsetting and—"

"A reminder," Zora added.

"I'm sorry, for what it's worth. I know he is, too. Felt sore after the drink wore off. Thought Jo might never speak to him again."

"Maybe she shouldn't," Zora challenged.

"Deep down, he's a good person."

Zora squirmed at the cliché. There were a lot of things deep down inside people: ugly things, sad things, devastating things. She thought Phillip wouldn't think what lurked deep down inside her was good.

"You go around making apologies for him?"

"Been doing it my whole life. Or at least since grade school. So please accept"—he pressed a hand dramatically to his chest—"my deepest and sincerest expression of regret."

The music started again. She noticed how he played along with his fingers along the table, as if they were memorizing each song. At times, he closed his eyes and bit his bottom lip. His hum was a rumble lingering just under each song.

She couldn't fight the pull, even though she knew she had to. Music or not, he was still a young white man. Trouble.

The set ended and the club began to close for the night.

"Can I drive you home?" he asked.

No.

No.

No.

"Yes," she replied.

They walked out of the club with the crowd. It had stopped raining. Zora felt the stares, but she tried not to look back at the people glaring at them.

"I'm parked over there." He pointed to the cherry-red car that was suddenly growing on her. "Got lucky tonight."

"You're rich." The words slipped out, and with them anxious flutters.

He opened the door for her. "My family is of means. But it isn't that simple."

She slid into the plush seats like the car was a too-hot bath. What was she doing? Her nerves were slipping and sliding inside her.

"Two-three-four-six North—"

"I know," he replied.

"You know where I live?" Zora eyed him. "So that *was* you that day. Outside the house."

His pale cheeks flushed pink. "I went on a very long walk. I ended up there."

"How do you just end up in places?" She studied his face, looking for the truth. "Especially colored neighborhoods you've got no business in."

"You ended up here in New Orleans."

The words settled over her, and she couldn't think of what to say back. He wasn't wrong. They rode the rest of the way in silence, stealing glances at each other. He turned onto Burgundy Street. There, a white man staggered around the street, slurring a song at the top of his lungs. He was missing his pants. Phillip stopped the car, and they watched as he danced and crooned, his verse asking where his pants might've disappeared to. Phillip's eyes found Zora's, and they burst with laughter.

"You think he's embarrassed?" he asked.

"Well, he's doing whatever he wants without caring what someone might say about it."

"Sounds like freedom," he said, turning onto Aunt Celine's street.

"All you need is a couple of bottles of hooch," she teased. "Then you could be out there, too. Dancing and singing. Without your pants on."

He laughed. "You want to see me making a fool of myself? Or just with my trousers off?"

An immediate flash of heat flared in Zora. "I didn't mean . . . I was just . . . What I meant was . . ." And then she laughed, a laugh she didn't think she still had inside her after all the things that had happened.

But then she remembered. It was bad enough for them to be seen together—to say nothing of flirting.

He parked out front and turned off the engine. The house was dark and quiet, and if she was in an admitting mood, she didn't want to go inside just yet. Thick raindrops started to hit the windshield.

"Another storm's coming," he said.

"It's always raining here." She watched the fat drops stretch into a lacy pattern across the glass.

"My father said the whole town is a lightning rod."

The rain drummed the roof.

"When I was a kid, I used to think it was God's music, his melody," he said, tracing his finger along the window as if he was trying to catch them. His words sent a buzz through her flesh. She'd never been around anyone outside her papa who loved music like she did.

"My papa used to say storms had a rhythm. That music comes from the natural order of things."

"You think God wanted there to be music?" Phillip asked. "You think he left the notes and beats behind for us to find?"

"My papa thinks God gave colored people jazz and the blues to deal with all the mess in this world. Gave them something to ease the pain. That it was our divine melody buried deep in our marrow," Zora said as the memory of her father's words washed over her like the rain outside the window.

"I believe that," he said. "It's the best music in the world. I can't go a day without listening to it. Really, any music. Classical, opera, country...though jazz is my favorite. I look for it and listen for it everywhere I go."

"So do I," Zora said.

"Can I ask you a question?" He bit his bottom lip, like he did when he was listening to a melody.

"I don't know, can you?" she said with a smile.

He laughed and turned bright red. He squeezed the steering wheel, fingers flickering with nerves. "Do you have...I mean...you must have many suitors."

She should say yes.

She should get out of the car right now.

She should never even entertain something so dangerous.

Instead, she laughed.

He turned even redder.

"What's funny?"

"Your assumptions about me."

"So you don't have suitors?"

"I don't."

His nervous hand found hers. She let him hold it, then lift it to his mouth. The warmth of his lips sent a ripple across her skin. "Can I kiss you?"

Part of her wanted to say no, to stop this—whatever it was—before it began. But words came out as effortlessly as the magic. "Isn't a kiss nothing more than music made between mouths?" she said.

Her *yes* was a tiny whisper that felt like a firework. She pressed her answer into his lips.

8

The next morning, Zora stood on her aunt's dress block with her hands pressed to her stomach, biting back a smile. Her lips still tingled with the memory of Phillip's mouth. She could still almost taste it.

The padded box sat in the middle of the close semicircle of mirrors in her aunt's dressmaking studio. A large worktable held patterns and scraps of fabric. A row of cloth mannequin dress forms held dresses in various stages of construction. Jars of bits and bobbles and thingamabobs and buttons and zippers cluttered the shelves. Folded fabric swatches were stacked in dangerous towers, and needles poked out of a hundred pincushions lined up on her desk. Spools of colorful thread filled a nearby shelf. The large hulking sewing machine sat near her desk, and a small bed was tucked in the corner.

Aunt Celine gazed up, catching her staring at the beautiful bed quilt. "Sometimes I work through the night on dress orders, and my bones get too heavy to drag up the stairs to my room," her aunt said through a mouthful of pins as she hunched over to hem the debutante gown. "You have the longest legs," she grumbled. "Much taller than both Ana and Evelyn. They got their height from their father. He was a bit short."

She didn't know much about her aunt's life because Celine Broussard was a person who didn't like memories. She'd tucked all the evidence of Germain Broussard away in locked steamer trunks. And she wasn't the kind of person who took too kindly to being badgered. Zora had stopped asking about him when all of her questions brought tears to both Ana and Evelyn's eyes. To Zora, he was a man in a black-and-white photograph—a man who wore a simple part in his hair and had light brown skin like hers; a man who had recently died.

Meanwhile, memories of her own parents seemed to slip further and further away like water down a drain the longer she was away from home.

Her aunt wore one of her long handmade dresses, blue, as always, and little-heeled shoes that left sores on her big toes when she wore them for too long. She'd twisted her hair into a bun pulled so tight that at first you wouldn't notice the curly texture or the shock of white at the crown. If Zora buried her face in her aunt's dress, she would smell the fanciest perfume and sweetest rose soap. Zora thought it reasonable to call her aunt beautiful.

"You seem different today," her aunt said. "Like you're finally settling in. Mama B's medicine must be working."

"Yes, Aunt Celine," she responded, trying not to smile too much.

Zora didn't want the fragile thread of excitement to snap. She listened as her aunt jumped around topics: how no one would have a dress like this one or the ones she'd made for Ana and Evelyn, how most girls wouldn't receive a call-out card or be able to dance with krewe members, how one of the girls had to pull out because her mother discovered she was pregnant.

Sometimes Zora wondered if secrets could grow like babies, pushing out your stomach and expanding until forced out. She imagined the twisted look of horror on her aunt's face if Zora ever told her something like that. Or if she ever found out that only hours ago, she sat right outside the house kissing Phillip Deveraux. A young white man. Someone it was illegal to even share space with, let alone kiss.

Zora suddenly wondered what it would be like to have a small person with little fingernails growing inside her. Would it have magic? Would the magic be musical like hers—even if Mama B removed it from her? Could it still be passed down like any other gene, eye shape or height or smile? Could it still do damage?

She suddenly wondered if Mama had had the same thoughts about having her.

"It'll be Mardi Gras season before you know it. Tomorrow is the first day of September, and whenever the fall shows up, it's a straight shot to Christmas and New Year's and then the krewe balls. So many dresses to make between now and then. I'm already tired."

"Tell me more about Mardi Gras and the krewe balls?" Zora asked. She'd tried so hard to ignore Ana and Evelyn, she realized, that she didn't know what she was in for.

"That's when all the societies throw the biggest and most smashing affairs, honey. They try to outdo each other with parade floats and parties. The colored folks have their own version over here in the back-a-town. But the white folks clog the streets. The *Voice* and the *Spokesman* papers will fill with all the debutantes, and the city will be one big fête. But if you don't stop fidgeting, I'll never get these measurements right."

"Sorry." It was as if her limbs couldn't stop humming with the memory of that kiss. She gazed at the closets of gowns and puffy wedding dresses and men's suits in another closet. The walls were bunched with so many orders in progress it made her feel like they were standing inside a pillow.

"Mardi Gras is when the city unleashes its monsters," Aunt Celine said with pins between her teeth. "The masks people wear all year come off; the things they keep inside all pour out. Like the good Lord knew we needed a few nights of sin to stay on the righteous path. There will be pretty costumes and beads and king cake and drinks. More than you could ever want—or need."

Zora didn't know what to think. Wild images of never-ending parties and overflowing glasses of champagne and revelers in the street all night filled her mind. But even then, she couldn't be sure what it would be like. She just knew she wanted to see it all, eat all the food, hear all the music, and collect all the beads.

"We will find you the right suitor," her aunt announced. "I know my girls love Christophe, but I've been thinking he'd make a good match for you. He's a lovely young man. His mother said he offered to show you around."

"Yes, ma'am, he did," she replied. Part of her looked forward to going to see other colored clubs, something she might never be able to do with Phillip. But Phillip's crooked smile popped into her head.

"You would make a nice couple. Very equally yoked."

Zora's muscles tightened. If this had been a week ago, she couldn't have seen herself with anyone. She'd never been one of the girls who'd dreamed of her wedding day, knowing the style of dress and what kind of cake she'd want. She only ever knew what new instrument she wanted to master playing and what next song she'd want to write. "Why not Ana or Evelyn?"

"My girls are still finding their way. You've got a few years on them. I still have some time to get them ready to be settled. They're so spoiled." She ruffled the muslin. "Marriage is a big responsibility— one they aren't quite ready for. Christophe Jr. will inherit his daddy's sugar business and needs a wife who has had some responsibilities in her life. Which you've had. But he has a good head on his shoulders. Is quiet and sweet. Steady, agreeable. You'd never want for anything. You'd be kept comfortable."

The way she spoke sounded like her life would be exactly like that of her cat's: sitting in a window, the days and weeks and months and years passing by without trouble. But she wanted adventure, laughter, and even to argue. Most of all, she wanted to be infused with music.

"It's a real chance at a fresh start. You need to find the right husband from the right family. That is key. A marriage is the joining of two families. They must find a way to fit like puzzle pieces. My Germain and I were fussy lovebirds. He liked to be in his own tree. I liked to be in mine, and we'd meet in the middle sometimes. But he understood me." She brushed a loose curl from her face, and Zora spotted a wayward tear. "No one will be perfect. But finding the right lovebird for yourself requires work."

"How did you know?" She eased the question out.

A smile twitched across her aunt's lips. "He was smug and handsome. I was sitting in Maude's Patisserie, sketching dresses and having a cup of tea. I was passing, too, so it was a risk for him to say something to me."

"And he took the risk?"

"Old coot slipped me a note."

Zora smiled. "Romantic."

She laughed. "Let him tell it, he could woo a fly."

Zora burned with a question. She began to speak, then stopped.

Aunt Celine's eyebrow lifted. "Spit it out."

"But how'd you *know*?"

"Know what?"

"That Uncle Germain was..." She didn't even really know what she was asking.

"Oh, that I fancied him?"

Zora nodded.

"That part's easy. You always know. You'll see once you spend more time with Christophe."

Zora bit her bottom lip.

"The hard part is letting them see you. Down-into-your-bones type of seeing. That's real love. What happens when the music is turned off? And everyone is tired and worn out. Do you still want to dance? I wanted to dance with Germain forever. Still would if he hadn't of up and died and left me so soon." This was the nicest her aunt had been to her since she'd arrived.

And just like that, there was a flash of the Aunt Celine Zora knew. She handed Zora a handkerchief. "Clean yourself up. Wipe off the sweat so it doesn't soil the dress."

"Yes, ma'am." She paused, hoping to recapture that easy banter from before. "I still don't understand why it's *this* hot. Back home the leaves would be turning by mid-September."

"Ah, New Orleans is a city that holds on to a lot of things, including heat." Aunt Celine dangled a towel. "We're going to add a bit of volume to this dress. I know the fashion is all drop waists and fringe and beads right now, but for the krewe balls . . . it's all about the pomp. The bigger, the better." She pointed to the partition screen in the corner. "Go take this off and come back. You can just wear your slip."

Zora went behind the partition screen and removed the muslin pattern. She ran the moist towels over herself once more to make sure she wouldn't soil whatever her aunt was digging out of the closet. Her aunt being nice to her felt good. The best she'd felt since she'd arrived.

Her aunt started to hum, and Zora joined in. With a huge hoop-skirt crinoline in her hands, her aunt motioned for her to step inside. She laced the skeleton of the bottom of a big eighteenth-century dress around Zora's waist. The bands were tight, squeezing her stomach.

"This is what they wear?" Zora asked.

"Welcome to New Orleans, petite. A place both backward and forward."

Zora crossed her hands over her chest.

"You've got nothing I don't already have. Let's see it." Her aunt laughed.

She shuffled around. The crinoline swayed around her waist. She climbed back on the box in the middle of the room.

Her aunt circled. She went to get all her standing mirrors, placing them around Zora.

Zora stared at the reflections of herself, going backward without end. She wondered if the person who looked back at her was actually who she was. If she'd be able to let Phillip see her. Or Christophe. Or anyone. She wondered if she would be able to love someone enough to still dance with them, even if the music went off. She wondered if she could be loved like that in return, even after what she'd done.

All those possibilities swirled inside her. The fear bubbling up, threatening to find its way out. The mirrors felt like they were inching forward on imaginary feet to enclose her in a glass prison. Sweat oozed from her pores despite her attempts to stay still. The sweat began to pool on her forehead and underarms.

Aunt Celine returned with a few large swatches of fabric. The waves swallowed her small frame. She stepped on the stool behind Zora's padded box.

"Wait, Aunt Celine." Zora tried to wipe herself again with the handkerchief.

"You hot?" she asked.

"I'm fine. I'll be fine." She suddenly wanted one thing to go well with her aunt. She wanted to show her that it wasn't a mistake to open up her home. She wanted to prove that she could do something right.

"Place these under your armpits." Aunt Celine folded two handkerchiefs into triangles and tucked them under Zora's arms. She blotted Zora's forehead and reached for a hand fan. Her motions created a small breeze.

"All right," she directed. "Hands up. We're going to try on this old dress of Ana's just to see if the style of it goes with your frame. You're shaped like your mama—I swear. You'll need a few more step-ins to get the latest look."

The handkerchiefs fell as Zora curled down some and her aunt slid the dress over her. The fabric scratched the skin on her sides.

"Now, we won't have it exactly like this because it's out of fashion . . .

but I just wanted to see the shape of things." She yanked the dress over the crinoline. She zipped it, the bodice choking Zora's rib cage. Aunt Celine admired Zora like a trinket, turning her on the dress block to see every side.

Zora tried to watch herself as she turned. It made her dizzy.

Her aunt took out her sketchbook and made notes, murmuring occasionally.

"I love this lace still. Beautiful beadwork, too."

"Maybe too much volume."

"The silhouette has aged, definitely. But you will be beautiful."

Zora found her reflection in the mirror. For the first time, she wanted someone to find her beautiful.

Later that evening, Zora sat at the kitchen table, helping Mabel peel a fifteen-pound bag of potatoes. She'd found Mabel crying that afternoon about how she'd never get it all done and how Madame Celine would punish her, maybe even fire her. It made Zora think about Mama and how an extra set of hands always made the work lighter.

Mabel swished in and out of the room, fretting over polished silverware and starched tablecloths. This time, Aunt Celine had invited a bunch of Holy Rollers. They would come with their church fans and Bibles, humming gospel music and talking about the sins of jazz, dancing, and alcohol. Of course, Aunt Celine had locked her wine and whiskey in the attic, far from their prying eyes.

The rhythm of peeling soothed her. The swish, swish, flick. Brown peels hitting the table like thick bandages.

There was a light knock at the back door.

"Sweet bean, will you get that?" Mabel called from the dining room. "Your aunt's expecting a delivery. Been paid for already. Just put it on the counter for me, will you?"

"Yes, ma'am," she replied.

Zora pulled the window curtain down to take a peek. She felt a brief pang of alarm.

It was Rocco. Phillip's friend. The one in love with Jo.

She opened the door—but only a few inches. "Can I help you?" she said, stone-faced.

He smiled with his greasy grin. "Hey, Zora. Remember me? Rocco Lucchese. Phillip's pal."

Zora kept the scowl on her face. There was still something about him that she didn't like. He hefted up a covered crate, and the sounds of kissing bottles echoed. Her alarm grew.

"Courtesy of the Fratello family," Rocco said. He stepped forward to carry them into the house, but Zora blocked his way. She felt a pinch of guilt. She knew what it was like to be judged based on the way that you looked, but there was something about him that she didn't trust.

"I'll take it." Zora had read in the papers about the Italian crime families and gangsters that had moved from New York City and Chicago to New Orleans. The Fratello family was the most notorious in the whole city. She'd seen the articles in the *Times-Picayune* about their various exploits. But she hadn't pictured Rocco. Where was his black suit? The hat? The cigar?

More important, how did someone like Phillip stay friends with someone like him?

"But it's heavy. I can bring it in," he said.

Zora took the crate from him. The weight of it almost knocked her over, but she grimaced and pretended it was light. "Thank you."

"No problem. Anything for our favorite customers."

She huffed to the table and placed the crate down. When she turned, he was still on the back doorstep. "My aunt said she already paid you."

"Oh, yes, she did. Very generous woman," he replied. "I was wondering if you could do me a favor?"

Zora crossed her arms over her chest. She motioned at the sack of potatoes. She wanted to bring this conversation to an end. "It depends on the favor," she said.

"Could you put a good word in for me with Jo?" he said. "Tell her I'm a nice guy?"

"But I don't know if that's true."

"Well, suppose I prove it to you." He took his hat off and pressed it to his chest. "She could make an honest man out of me."

"She's not here to fix you," Zora replied, irritated.

His face crumpled. "That's not what I meant."

"Then say what you mean."

"I think I'm falling in love with her. I know it hasn't been long, but..." He clutched his heart. "If you could ask her to give me a chance, a real one, I'd be forever grateful. I'm not no grifter or cake-eater, I'd be faithful to her and only her." His pleas felt genuine and sweet, but she still thought Jo deserved the very best—which wasn't Rocco.

She started to close the door in his face, but he reached out to stop her.

"I have something for you ... and it might make that whole favor thing easier," he said, that greasy smile showing itself again. He pulled an envelope from his pocket. "It's from Phillip. We're going out tonight. Jo, too."

Her heart jumped up into her throat. She reached for the letter, her fingers tingling. "Where?"

"The Orleans Roof Garden." He pulled it back just out of reach. "Meet us later?"

Her fingers itched for the letter. "Yes." He handed it over.

Zora waited until she couldn't see the back of Rocco's head as he disappeared down the block. She rushed to the kitchen door and gazed down the hall. No sight of Mabel or her aunt or even Ana or Evelyn.

Calm down, she told herself.

The magic inside her flared, and a note or two escaped.

She eased into the pantry, leaving the door cracked open for a sliver of light. Her fingers fumbled with the envelope. The paper was nice, expensive even, and the color of eggshells.

Zora,

Please meet us at Orleans Rooftop around 8 p.m. tonight. I promise I won't sing in the streets. I won't dance without music. Though I can dance. A little. Most of all, I promise to wear trousers.

Phillip

"Zora, honey," Mabel called out, barreling into the kitchen. "Bring me the paprika."

She pressed the letter to her chest and took a deep breath. "Yes, ma'am."

9

At eight on the dot, Zora met Jo outside the Orleans Roof Garden. The music rained down on them as they made their way to the front entrance. Zora's heart leapt, the magic tingling, nearly escaping out of her hands.

She was still confused about why Jo had agreed to go to this place. "Don't you hate the owner?" she asked Jo.

"Yes, but he's not here on Thursdays, and it's easier...you know... about *things*."

Zora knew that meant colored and white folks mixing about.

"Besides, I couldn't wait to see what the night had in store...." Jo batted her mischievous eyes at Zora. Big and impossible to deny. "You look beautiful," she added, holding Zora's hand as they rode the lift up to the roof.

"So do you," Zora answered, fingering the beads on the neckline of Jo's golden dress. Zora had tried on six different dresses before settling on this buttercup-yellow drop waist she'd sneaked out of her aunt's dress room. She just had to make sure not to spill anything on it tonight so she could sneak it back.

"Someone asked me to put in a good word for you today," Zora reported.

Jo's hazel eyes opened wide with surprise and excitement. "Who?"

"Rocco."

She blushed. "Really?"

"Yes, and the only reason I agreed to come tonight was—"

"Because you like Phillip." Jo burst into a fit of laughter. "Admit it. 'Cause if you try to lie to me, I'll throttle you."

Zora fought away a smile as the elevator made a stop and let some other folks in. She held her secret feelings for Phillip like they were a precious gem. She didn't want them exposed to the public yet. They'd be sullied. Because a relationship between the two of them was decidedly not allowed.

"Actually I came to watch out for *you*," Zora said. "What does Rocco do for a living?"

"Family business." Jo stiffened. "At least that's what he told me. I don't suppose you know what *Phillip* does? Since you want to be so nosy and act like my maman."

"I don't," Zora replied.

"Rocco said something about him working for his father, too. Shipping and sugar and cotton brokerage down on Canal Street, I think it is," Jo told her. "Phillip has a great job."

"I guess that's how he bought that gaudy red car."

"Oh, so you two have talked? When were you going to tell me?" Jo gave Zora an amused glance.

"Maybe just a little. But Rocco is bootlegging and God knows what else. He's a criminal." The words felt sharp and sour on her tongue, the taste of hypocrisy. She was a criminal, too. She'd hurt someone and was hiding from the consequences of it.

"I mind my business about that sort of thing, Zora, and so should you. Can't go around accusing people of things, especially when you don't *really* know. Plus, he said he was striking out on his own soon." She squeezed Zora's hand tighter. "But what did he say about *me*?"

I think I'm falling in love with her. Zora frowned. She didn't want Jo to get hurt. "Just that he liked you."

"He does?" Her eyes brightened. She was even more beautiful when excited.

"You knew that already," Zora said, squeezing back.

"Yes, but it's one thing to think it and another thing for him to say it. Why didn't you call me immediately?" she squealed. "Or run over."

"I'm not a messenger pigeon," Zora teased. "It happened this afternoon, and I knew I'd be seeing you tonight. Don't get all huffy. Plus, my aunt doesn't like people using her telephone." She pinched the bridge of her nose and did her best impression. "It's for emergencies only . . . or emergency gossip."

The elevator porter cut them a look. Jo shushed Zora, but they broke into a fit of giggles. He quickly swept them up and onto the roof.

The gardens spread out before them. Large trees that belonged in the bayou stretched overhead, their lacy moss creating a canopy. Clusters of lanterns dropped from their branches like lightning bugs trapped in glass boxes. Well-dressed waiters carried platters of mouthwatering food from table to table. A fat moon cast its watery light over all the candlelit tables, and the band on the platform glistened—their dark hands rubbing against brass instruments that looked like they'd been fashioned from molten gold.

"We should've come early," Zora complained. "The colored section is probably already full."

"We have a table." Jo grabbed her hand and led her forward, zigzagging left and right, then left again as she navigated the heavy crowds and tables of curious white folks.

"How?"

"Just wait." Jo flashed a smile at her.

The music shone through Zora, momentarily quieting all of her worries and disappointments and troubles. The notes whispered to the magic inside her, making her hands warm and her veins swell with excitement.

Jo dragged her to the very front, stopping at a table where two young white men sat.

Rocco and Phillip.

The eyes from the white and colored sections found them. Zora felt a deep blush set into her cheeks—both from the sight of Phillip and the staring crowd. Looking around the Orleans Roof Garden at all the gawking eyes, she was reminded of the facts. They'd never *actually* be able to be together. She was colored. He was white. It was illegal. She had terrible magic inside her. He didn't know who she really was and what she had done.

"Jo," Zora whispered hard. "What are you doing?"

"They got us a table. Phillip's father has an investment in this place."

"We shouldn't." Zora tugged at her hand.

"We were *meeting* them here. What did you think that meant?"

Zora's heart backflipped. She actually didn't know. Seemed she'd gotten carried away with it all. "I thought ... thought we'd sit and listen at our own table and see them afterward ... or I don't know ..."

The young men stood to greet them and pulled out chairs for them to sit. People gasped from nearby tables.

Zora flushed. Phillip looked around as if challenging anyone to say anything.

But no one did.

A waiter brought drinks and everything continued on.

Zora slid into her chair, her anxiety dissipating a little. She tried to pretend that she wasn't bubbling over with a mix of terror and joy at seeing him.

"Good to see you again," Phillip said, his mouth parting in the widest grin. His blue eyes held a smile, the corners curling up. He wore a beautiful summer suit and a collarless shirt with one button open. She spotted the pale blond fuzz on his chest.

"And you," Zora replied. Her lips tingled with the memory of their kiss, wanting another.

"Have you seen Armand's Creole Band before? The way Theo there plays his trumpet makes me want to quit and never play again."

"Maybe you should. One less bad player bastardizing the best music in the whole world. Would keep it safe."

He scoffed with mock upset. "But you've never heard me play the trumpet."

"I value my ears. I suspect they might bleed."

He laughed, and she laughed, too. She had to admit it: She liked him. He was a little bit funny, a little bit handsome, and a little bit cocky. Zora didn't know what she planned to do about it, but for now, she couldn't stop exploring the what-ifs and maybes.

His hand brushed hers under the table. She reached for his fingers and intertwined them with hers. Phillip traced music notes into her palm and tapped the rhythm of the song. The warmth of his touch made her head light, and she thought she might float right off the rooftop and up to the stars.

"Where's the waiter?" Rocco barked, spoiling the mood. "We need more drinks."

"Calm down." Phillip put a hand on his shoulder. "It's swamped tonight." He craned his neck to look.

Rocco lifted Jo's empty glass. "I can't let my girl sit here without everything she wants."

Jo giggled. "I need extra cherries."

"Let's go order." Phillip took Rocco away from the table and smiled at Zora over his shoulder.

Her hand felt cold now without his.

As soon as the men were out of earshot, Jo leaned in. "You *really* like him."

"I don't like anyone but you," she lied.

"Oh, I can tell," Jo teased, and poked Zora's side. "You were laughing and smiling."

"Laughing *at* him is more like it. There's a difference." She wanted to be honest with Jo, pour out how she felt caught up in a storm of unknown feelings around him, but her fears were just as loud.

"Um-hmm. Keep telling the lies. Your nose'll be so big we won't be able to get back in that elevator."

"What about you and Rocco?" Zora asked.

"My mama would never approve, but it's fun for now."

"Because he's white?"

"We'd never be able to marry. It's still illegal. We'd be living in sin," Jo said. "She wants me with someone who has a house that she can come live in. Swept straight out of old Storyville."

"You can pass for white, though," Zora pushed.

"So could Homer Plessy, and he still couldn't sit in the whites-only car. And I wouldn't want to sign up for a life of passé-blanc. It's too hard. I'd be nervous to have children. I'd be looking over my shoulder every minute, waiting for the law to show up and take us."

Zora didn't want to live like that either. Hiding forever.

"Isn't your daddy white?" Zora said neutrally, trying not to offend.

"But he didn't marry Maman. He has another family over in a big fancy house in the Garden District. His *real* family. It's what people do down here. They just don't really talk about it."

She thought of her grandparents, one brown and one white. About how she didn't know any of her grandmother's family back in Germany. How Oma never spoke about her life in Hanau. She couldn't imagine Oma having her mother and her aunts and then disappearing or just coming around every so often. What would her life have been like? Weekly visits from Oma? The children raised by her grandfather? She thought about everything her oma and grandpa must have had to overcome because they loved each other.

"It's complicated." Jo swallowed the next part of her sentence.

A drunk white man in an expertly tailored suit stumbled over. "If I had known my sweet was going to be here tonight, I would've come earlier," he slurred out.

Jo shrank back. "Hello, Mr. Brodeur." There was a tremor of discomfort in her voice, making it quiver. Panic rose in Zora. The owner. The ogling man who always came into the Petit Sapphire. The owner who wasn't supposed to be here tonight.

"Why so formal? I told you to call me Jacques." He slid into the chair beside her, and she did her best to squirm away. "Don't run from me, my little bird."

Zora tried to speak firmly, but not so angrily people would look. "Those seats are taken."

"I own every seat in this place, girl. You shouldn't even be sitting here. Wouldn't have been able to if I hadn't allowed it." His droopy eyes combed over her. "And who is your pretty friend, little bird?"

Jo gulped. "This is Zora Broussard."

"Ah, and are you the Sweet Willow who sings at Petit Sapphire and not at my fine establishment?" He waved his hands all around. "You have to admit, mine is the better venue. Let me know if you fancy it and maybe we can make some arrangements. Especially if this one sings with you. I'd fill every seat in the house." He reached for Zora's hand, and she pulled it back. "But the best part is that I'd get to see you every night. Name your price."

"We're not for sale, sir," Zora said.

He smiled. "Everyone is."

Jo released nervous laughter.

"Zora, is it? I've been trying to get your sweet friend here to go out with me, but she always has an excuse. She's busy working or her mama won't let her or she's sick. Yet here she is tonight . . . and on the day I took off. Feels curious to me." He tapped his temple with his big white finger. "But luckily, I told my staff to ring me whenever you came, little bird, because I always have to see you. Better than a hot beignet fresh from the oil." He reached to touch Jo's hair, and she flinched, craning away from his touch. "Delicious, hot, and sweet.

"She plays this game with me, Sweet Willow. I'm the cat and she's the mouse. It drives me wild . . . almost mad." He glared at Jo until she pinkened. "She knows I love it. The thrill of winning. It's why I buy so many clubs and restaurants and hotels. I want my own little world carved out of this city."

Zora steadied her voice and squared her shoulders. "Sir, I assure you, she's not playing any game."

His eyes narrowed to slits. "What did you say to me, girl?"

"With all due respect, sir, I am not a girl." Anger flared and woke the magic inside her. It rumbled and bubbled to the surface. Her fingertips warmed as it prepared to explode out of her.

She tried to take a deep breath.

She tried to focus.

She tried to remain calm.

He touched Zora's arm. "She teases me. Don't you think that's wrong?"

Zora pulled away. He turned back to a petrified Jo.

"You worried 'cause you're colored and I'm not?" He leaned closer. "You don't have to. Plenty folks around here skate around that. I'd find a way. Always preferred brown sugar, anyway."

Zora opened her mouth to challenge him, but Jo put a hand on hers.

"I'm so sorry, Mr. Brodeur," Jo said in her most honeyed voice— the one that could get anything out of any man. "I really do appreciate your flattery. But my mama doesn't allow me to be courted."

"Then who is he?" He turned and pointed at the backs of Rocco and Phillip at the bar, his face reddening with anger. "Tell me who he is right now." Before Jo could respond, he slapped her across the face. "You're nothing but a colored harlot like your maman." He yanked her hair and brought her swollen mouth to his. "Leading me on. Denying me a single taste."

Zora's mind swirled, and her temper unleashed. Veins in her face, hands, arms, and legs rose to the surface of her skin and revealed a roadmap of magic paths through her body. Her pulse raced. She closed her eyes for a moment, and in the darkness her own magic flashed like heated tentacles. The fine hairs on her arms stood up, warning of an imminent strike. She couldn't bottle her anger.

She couldn't keep it in.

The roof's candles snuffed out, blanketing everything in darkness.

Her magic poured out of her like lightning, the music notes lengthening to bolts and stretching and pulsing into a tree of black light. The threads rearranged into a spiderweb and caught the man, prying him off Jo.

She tossed him left and right, snapping his leg as easily as a tree branch caught in a terrible storm.

10

The whole rooftop became a tangle of chaos. Women and men ran in a thousand directions. The elevators flooded with people. Tables overturned. Glasses broke into a mosaic of shattered bits and pieces. A chorus of screams cut through the night.

Zora dropped to her knees and willed herself to stop. Phillip rushed to her side. She felt his strong hands on her waist.

"What happened? Are you all right?" He helped her to stand and gave her a handkerchief.

SHATTERED MIDNIGHT

Did he see what I did?

She could feel blood gushing from her nose and down her neck. "Where's Jo?" Zora said. Her whole body shook, and her legs felt like they might give out at any minute. She put the handkerchief to her face to stop the crimson stream. "Is she all right?"

"Rocco went with her into the stairwell. We should go. Now!" She allowed him to help her push through the throng of bodies. "This way."

They hustled down ten flights of stairs with a crowd of upset and terrified people. By the time they reached the street, many were already tending to the wounded, and a bloody and drunken Mr. Brodeur was carried out on a stretcher. Police held notepads and pens and rounded up groups to take statements. Everyone poured into the lobby, where medics and police officers waited.

Zora and Jo spotted each other in the chaos. They met in the middle of the room, losing the boys in the sea of people, and squeezed each other tight. Zora didn't want to let her go. She stroked Jo's swollen cheek. "Are you sure you're all right? I can't believe he . . ."

"I'm fine. I'm fine." Jo panted, her voice hoarse from screaming and crying. "But are you?" She pulled back and looked into Zora's eyes, then glanced at the bloodied handkerchief she was pressing against her nose. "What happened? All I saw was the table flipping. The candles blowing out. My ears are still ringing from all the screaming."

Zora's mind raced and her eyes darted all around. She could barely hear Jo over all the noise in the room and the sound of her pounding heartbeat flooding her ears. "I think I shoved the table. It was so dark, and that storm started..." she began to lie. "I'm not sure what happened. I was just so angry that he touched you."

This would be how she'd be caught. She was certain of it. She'd be arrested, her identity exposed, and her mama's veil would be all for nothing.

She felt eyes on her as people pointed in her direction. Her whole body tingled, a mix of adrenaline, fear, and magic. What would she say to them? How would she explain it?

Jo started to cry, and Zora wrapped her arms tighter around her as if to absorb all of it, careful not to get any blood on her. She felt the heat trapped in Jo's swollen cheek. "We have to go." Zora started to walk toward the door.

A cop stepped into their path, stopping them.

"Excuse me, Miss..."

"Broussard. Zora Broussard," she answered.

"May I have a word with you?"

"She didn't do anything," Jo interjected.

"I didn't say she did," the policeman replied, his face twisting with irritation and suspicion. "And who are you?"

"Josephine Robichaux, sir."

"We were just leaving, sir," Zora replied.

"Not until I say so."

Zora clenched her jaw.

"Where were you when Mr. Brodeur was injured?" he asked Zora.

"At our table," Zora replied.

"And which table was that?"

How should I know? "Near—near the band, toward the left."

His eyes narrowed. "And?"

"And what, sir?"

"You sure are eager to leave. Did you cause this trouble?" His doughy white cheeks flushed red.

"We don't cause trouble," Zora told him.

"All you people do is make a mess."

Anger hardened inside her, but she smiled.

"Don't play with me," the officer said. "I'll make it so—"

"He was touching me. He hit me," Jo blurted out, showing him her swollen lip and eye. "It was all my fault." She burst into tears again. "He fancies me, and I keep rejecting his advances."

His blond eyebrow lifted. "I find it hard to believe that a rich man such as Jacques Brodeur would go to all this trouble for a ..." He frowned.

Zora braced for him to say the words *colored woman* or worse. To insinuate that a rich white man would never be interested in such a woman like Jo ... or like herself.

Phillip strode over, inserting himself. "Jacques Brodeur has a notorious womanizing reputation, Officer." He stood between the girls and the policeman. "I defended them from his inappropriate and aggressive advances. We got into a fistfight. This spilled out and caused a ruckus. My apologies."

Jo began to sob, and Zora squeezed her tight.

"And just who are you?"

"Phillip Deveraux Jr."

"Oh." The policeman reached out to shake his hand. "I knew Big Phillip had a son, but I hadn't had the pleasure."

The policeman's voice softened. He took off his hat and smiled at Phillip as if he could've been his very own son. More anger piled up inside Zora as the policeman listed all the things he loved about Phillip's father. She stormed off. Jo followed behind her, and then Rocco. She had to get some air.

The street buzzed with onlookers and those telling their version of what happened to lurking newspaper reporters and journalists, and the occasional nosy neighborhood person.

"Zora, it'll be all right," Jo called out.

"Give me a minute." Zora moved away from the group, pressing her hands to her stomach, and tried to catch her breath. She thought of all the terrible things she wanted to tell that policeman.

She told herself not to cry.

She told herself that no one died this time.

She told herself that it was a mistake.

Another one.

She bit down on her lip to keep it from quivering and fanned her hands in front of her eyes to stop the threat of tears. One thing was certain—she could not let something like that happen again. She would meet Mama B next month and get rid of the magic. No matter the cost.

"Zora."

She whipped around to find Phillip.

"You all right?"

Her anger snapped loose. "I didn't need your help," she spat.

"I know."

"What do you *really* know?"

His forehead crinkled with surprise. "That officer nearly killed a German man out in Jefferson parish last year for sassing him. Once, he strung up a nine-year-old by the thumbs until he confessed to stealing pralines in the French Quarter. He's not someone to play with."

Her fury softened a little, like butter first set out on the counter for baking. "How do you know all of that?"

"Rocco. Apparently the officer's been nosing around some of his business dealings, so Rocco made a point of finding out more about *him*."

"Don't save me. I'm not a trapped cat," she said.

He paused. "I was thinking of us more like wolves. They mate for life, protect their pack. Maybe we can save each other."

"I'm not a wolf either." She refused to laugh at his absurdity, at his clever smile.

"But they're beautiful."

"And they have sharp teeth." Zora gave her best frown even though her mouth was starting to fight it, wanting to return his easy grin.

The crowd thinned out behind them, the policemen returning to their station. Rocco leaned into Phillip's car, holding Jo, stroking her back until her hiccuping sobs ceased. Zora watched how tightly he held her, and she suddenly got the feeling he wouldn't let her fall. Maybe he did love her. Maybe she'd judged him too soon.

"Zora, I am sorry if I offended." Phillip jammed his hands in his pockets. "I wanted to help. Do you forgive me?"

"Maybe," she replied, releasing a deep breath. The stress of the night drifted off little by little like a storm being pulled out to sea. The pulse of the magic still lingered just under her skin.

"Everything's a maybe with you."

"It's my favorite word."

He smiled, and she smiled back right away this time.

"Want a ride home?"

"I'll walk."

He looked crestfallen.

"My feet don't need saving tonight either." She started to move ahead, but he touched her hand. His touch took the sting out of her. "Please. I'll walk with you."

Zora's whole body said yes even though her mind protested. She was out of control, and she shouldn't drag him into it. Tonight proved it. Tonight was a reminder. Tonight was a warning. But she nodded. Phillip told Rocco to take Jo home in the car and to meet him later.

Zora and Phillip walked in silence for several blocks, skipping over puddles of sewage and sidewalks soaked from an earlier rain. The tea and honey biscuits she'd had churned in her stomach, threatening to come up. She swallowed against the stench of a hot night: the crawfish edging on rotten, the alcohol verging on sour. The perfume and cologne most wore to mask their sweat turned acrid.

The adrenaline had left her body by the time they reached the end of St. Louis Street. The entrance to the St. Louis Cemetery No. 1 stood before them. Soon she'd be here with Mama B, and nothing like what happened tonight would ever happen again.

"I know." Phillip broke the silence.

Zora looked up at him. Moonlight made his pale eyes glow. "Know what?" Her thoughts raced.

"I know you have a secret."

Tears came to her eyes. She could just say *magic* out loud. She could admit it. Then she would just be free of this.

"I have a secret, too." He brushed a tear from her cheek with the pad of his thumb. "I've seen your shoes before."

She hadn't expected that. She looked down at Oma's red T-straps. "What do you mean?"

"I've seen them on a woman ... in a vision," he said. He squeezed her tight. "I know it sounds ridiculous."

She wanted to answer *Nothing you could say would sound ridiculous.*

"How?" she asked.

"My family has a special mirror," he said. "It's been passed down to me." He ran a hand through his hair. "It shows me things. Sometimes the future, sometimes the past."

A magic mirror? She studied him. Was *he* like her? How could this be? Zora balled her fists to keep her hands from shaking.

"When I was a child, sometimes I'd see images that didn't make sense. I saw my mother use it, too. Asking about business affairs I didn't know much about or if a relative would survive an illness," he said. "I think it drove her mad."

"Why not destroy it?"

He shrugged. "She wouldn't allow it. Said it protected the family. Said it was the most important part of my inheritance."

Zora glanced down at her red shoes again. What were her grandmother's secrets? How did they connect to all the bad things that had happened?

"Sometimes I get visions in other types of reflections, too—on windows, shiny things, my car..." he said. "I saw you and your house a few times. The images kept flashing for me no matter where I was. That's why I walked there that day," he admitted. "I'd seen it. I needed to know why."

She felt the panic coursing through her body.

"I don't know what it means, but I feel like it means we're supposed to be together. That I'm supposed to protect you."

Zora's heartbeat consumed her entire body. "Why? Phillip..."

He looked away from her. The cemetery gates glimmered in the moonlight, and the cicadas started a rousing chorus, filling the thick air with their music.

"The woman with my shoes—the one in your vision. What's she doing?"

Phillip looked at her. "She's in a coffin."

September 15, 1928

Dear Zora,

I know you can save yourself.

Just for the record ... you're more beautiful than a wolf.

Phillip

September 20, 1928

Dear Zora,

You should write me back. At least so I can see if your handwriting is as great as mine.

Phillip

October 1, 1928

Dear Phillip,

My handwriting is decidedly better than yours.

Zora

11

*T*he hot sticky summer tumbled into fall, and September turned to October. There were no leaves to change to orange and butterscotch and burnt red, but a damp cool started to blanket the city at night. A breeze found its way through the open windows as she sat in the sitting room with her aunt and Christophe Bechet Jr. finishing up tea.

"Yes, ma'am, I promise to have her back on time." Zora's eyes darted from Christophe to Aunt Celine to Ana. She'd told her cousin they were just going on a long walk so he could show her around New Orleans.

Christophe set his teacup down and submitted to Aunt Celine's interrogation while Ana sulked in the doorway. He looked handsome in white trousers and a navy blazer and boater hat. She could see why many girls would like him. Away from his insufferably stuffy parents, he wasn't so bad.

He just wasn't Phillip.

"You stay out of unsavory places, you hear?" Aunt Celine said with a smile. "I know how wonderfully your parents have raised you, so I just say this as a reminder."

"Yes, ma'am," he replied, then turned to Zora. "Are you ready?"

They slipped out, Ana's whiny voice following them. "Maman..."

"I would never want to cross your aunt," he said with a chuckle, a warm smile exposing one small dimple in his left cheek.

"She's tough, that's for sure." Zora gazed back at the house and spotted Ana's face in the window. She planned to make it up to her somehow if only so she wouldn't have to hear her mouth.

Zora and Christophe walked toward the French Quarter, passing shotgun homes sitting like rows of colorful gingerbread houses. People lingered on porches or in the street, playing dominoes or making music. The city was always alive, but in a different way from back home: While the folks in that northern city hustled and bustled, those down here relished the heat and good drinks and music. Here, warmth made everyone a little slower.

"Everyone's always outside," she said.

"Trying to catch a breeze and a tune," he replied.

"Will they do this even when it gets cold?" Zora admired a young boy thrumming a washboard and singing a song.

"It never gets *cold* cold."

They turned right to avoid a second line parade. Zora gazed back at the dancing revelers, wishing she could join them.

"Your cousin Evelyn said you love those."

"I do. We don't have them in New York City."

"Wait until Mardi Gras season starts. You'll get sick of them quick."

"I could never." Her heart fluttered at the thought. She'd imagined it like the Macy's Thanksgiving Day Parade but even bigger and better.

"We love our parties. It'll be beads and feathers and booze everywhere for weeks," he said. "The carnival queens will fill up the papers."

"The queens?"

"Most beautiful and popular women from the different social clubs. Bet the Original Carolina Club will choose you."

Zora gulped and felt her cheeks warm. "I doubt that. I'm new, after all."

"That's why," he said with a wink, turning left down another street. "Sometimes they like a surprise to keep everyone on their toes." He led Zora forward, helping her step over a puddle to keep her T-straps pristine. "If I could cast a vote, it'd be for you."

"You have to say that," Zora replied.

"I probably shouldn't. We're just getting to know each other." Christophe looked away. "My parents are keen on you."

"Why? I didn't think I made that great of an impression at my aunt's dinner." Embarrassment from that night washed over her again. The shattered glass. "I was having a bad night."

"My father was amused. You're someone who speaks her mind. He says that's rare in a person. That most people show only a side of themselves that they think others want to see." Christophe mopped his sweaty brow with a handkerchief. "But you're honest, to a fault. Or you were that night. You have pride and integrity, and what's more important than that?"

Zora's stomach squeezed. If he only knew how many lies she was telling and the mask she wore. . . .

"Look," he said, pointing.

Rows of jazz clubs lined the street, music pouring out from each one. Well-dressed colored people ducked in and out of them. Zora hadn't walked down this street before. There was so much about this city still ripe for discovery. She felt Christophe's eyes on her as she took it all in.

"This is . . ." The words stuck to the roof of her mouth.

"Definitely something." He walked forward and reached back for her hand.

Zora paused, unsure how she could refuse, thinking of Phillip before taking it. There was a pinch of guilt in her chest as she slipped her palm into his and walked forward with him.

Christophe told her the history of every single club as if they were in a museum and he was a docent. She loved the little details, like which ones got shut down for bootlegging or the ones that all the performers loved the most or the ones that always had a fight in them. She couldn't wait to visit them all.

"I can't believe I've never heard of any of these," she said.

"Gets a little rough at night, so I wouldn't expect a lady to patronize any of these businesses."

"I'm not that much of a lady."

"The Petit Sapphire is only three blocks up." Christophe stopped at a street vendor selling pralines beside an alley. "Want some?"

"Sure," she replied.

As he fished a few coins from his pocket, Zora wandered a little away, her eyes taking in the sights while she listened to the music pouring out of all the venues.

Angry voices echoed and pulled her attention from the alley, and Zora craned to look at the side door of a nearby club jammed open.

She was shocked to see Rocco there, arguing with two large red-faced white men. Their brimmed hats shaded their eyes and made them look terrifying in the twilight.

While Christophe talked to the vendor, she tucked herself into the shadows and watched.

"You told me you'd have the money," one said to Rocco, a cheroot cigar hanging from his lip.

"I promise you it's coming, Cosimo," Rocco said, a plea in the bass of his voice.

"You're full of promises, kid," the other one replied. "The only reason we haven't cracked your skull like an egg is 'cause your uncle says to give you another shot. You owe us. You been owing us."

"Frankie, I know, I know. I got it coming."

"We want less of *it's coming*...and more of *it's here*." The bigger one flicked the fiery end of his cigar in Rocco's direction. "If we have to come looking for you to collect, it's going to be the last time anybody sees you. You hear me?"

Rocco nodded.

What do they want from him? she wondered. *What kind of trouble is he in?*

"Zora." Christophe called her name, pulling her back toward him. "What's going on?"

"I thought I saw a rat," she lied as her mind buzzed with worries. Mostly for Jo and what would happen if she did decide to be with Rocco. How would he keep her safe? He owed men debts. They would collect them. Jo wouldn't be safe. "What time is it?"

"Half past eight," he said after clicking his pocket watch open.

Almost time for her to meet Phillip at the club.

"I'm late getting back home. My aunt will be upset."

"Your aunt loves me."

"Maybe so, but I don't want to test her. We should walk back."

Christophe smiled and nodded. "Yes, you're right. I want to stay in her good graces so she allows me to go out with you again."

Being out with him wasn't so bad. It felt comfortable—like spending time with an old friend. Not at all what she expected. They walked back, eating pralines and talking. She let him walk her to the porch and kiss her on the cheek.

"I had a lovely evening," he said.

"So did I," she replied, which was the surprising truth.

She waved and waited for Christophe to disappear around the corner before going in and showing her face for dinner, only to pretend to be sick so she could head to the Petit Sapphire to meet Phillip.

Zora eased into the Petit Sapphire. The excitement made her almost vibrate. She wanted as much time as possible to go over the sheet music and rehearse a bit on the piano in the dressing room. She wanted it to be perfect. Her performing days were numbered. But she didn't want to think about all that tonight.

The usual suspects greeted her as she made her way to the back of the club. She navigated dark corridors and passed Miles's office. She was so wrapped up in her storm of thoughts she didn't hear Phillip slip into the room.

His scent wrapped all around her, along with his arms.

"You're already here," she said.

"I am," he replied, the words hitting her neck.

Zora sank back into him, the warmth of his body around her like a glove. He held out a little bouquet of flowers, star-shaped and white; its scent filled the room. "What's that?"

"For you . . ."

Her heart squeezed.

"These are sort of special in my family. On our crest." His arms wrapped around her tighter.

"Your what?" There were so many things they didn't know about each other, and Zora was nervous to peel back the layers and find things that would further push them apart. There was already a mountain of trouble they'd have to face if anyone found out that they were spending time together.

"Brought all the way from Germany." He twirled her around to face him. "Where were you? I've been waiting.... Well, to be more accurate, I've been pacing out back like a terrified dog." He lowered his voice, his eyes worried. "I have to admit—that image in the mirror has been haunting me. Every time I see it, I wonder what it means.... If you—"

Zora kissed his cheek, touched that he was so concerned. "I'm completely fine. See?" She spun around again. "I had to have tea with my aunt and then had to entertain one of the suitors she arranged," she said. "Please don't worry."

"Ah, it seems both of us have had demands put upon us."

"You too?"

"My father. It seems now is the time he's decided to get involved with the particulars of my life. Wants me to take over the family shipping and brokerage business and marry a girl from an upstanding family. Even set up a date with the daughter of one of his clients."

Zora stiffened, knowing full well that she was being silly, that she'd just told him about another boy, after all. "And your mother?"

He sighed. "She keeps to herself mostly, doesn't talk much. But when she does, it's usually to agree with him. Or say something about our bad luck."

Zora thought about the sanatoriums he'd mentioned before. She changed the subject. "How was the date?"

Phillip grinned. "I was a perfect ass, so Lady Charlotte du Caron is no longer interested." He tucked one of the star-shaped flowers into her thick bob. "They suit you—a star for a star. They'll remind me of you now." He kissed her cheek, still warm from Christophe.

The sound of Rocco's shouting stamped out the rest of his kiss. Zora flinched and tried to move away from Phillip.

"No one is coming in. I locked it," he assured her.

But she still felt uneasy.

"What's wrong? There's plenty of time before you have to go on."

"It's not that." She weighed whether to say anything. "It's Rocco."

"What'd he do this time?"

"I saw him earlier while out on a walk. He was talking to some strange men."

"Well, he's a bit odd himself," he said, trying to get her to laugh.

"They were threatening him about money."

Phillip frowned. "He's always in some mess that I have to help dig him out of."

"It sounded bad. Dangerous, even."

"Bootlegging is."

"You both are so different."

He touched her cheek. "So are we."

"I mean that he seems to flirt with trouble . . . and you don't."

"What would you call this?" Phillip started to leave a trail of soft kisses from the crook of her neck to the top of her forehead.

"I'm serious," Zora fussed.

He paused and looked up at her. "He's a person who wants to get ahead. Is selling illegal alcohol the right thing to do? Maybe not. But we all do things that aren't the right thing in the moment."

His touch started to soften her hard edges. She knew a lot about decisions like that. "I stay out of his business and he stays out of mine. I try not to judge him. But I wouldn't keep him close if I couldn't trust him, if I didn't feel like he was safe."

Her eyes closed with a flutter as he left more kisses down the other side of her face and neck. "I worry for Jo."

"You should be worried about me showing you up tonight when I'm on the piano." He nibbled her neck and she squealed.

"You're playing with us again?" she asked.

A smile played across his mouth. "I have some news . . . but you have to pretend you don't know when Jo and Miles tell you. They wanted it to be a surprise."

"What is it?"

"For a kiss. That's the price."

She rolled her eyes in mock upset and let her mouth brush against his. "Now . . . tell me."

He bit his bottom lip. "Red ran off. Guess he owed somebody and has to lay low for a little bit, so I offered to play with you and Jo until he gets back."

A deep flicker of happiness ignited inside her.

12

*T*he days sailed by like quick fingers across smooth white piano keys. Zora sang and played with Phillip and Jo as much as she could, wanting to soak up every single piece of music before she'd have to see Mama B. If a band called out sick, she filled in. The three of them fell into an endless rhythm, a song none of them wanted to end. Zora would sneak out early to meet Phillip and Jo in the dressing room at the back of the club, where they'd go through sheet music, prepare for their set, and even write new songs together. Each night, the crowd swelled, packing every table in the club with eager listeners there to hear Sweet Willow, Jo, and their white boy on piano, and just before sunrise, Phillip would drop her off and she'd tiptoe back into her aunt's house in her little red shoes and slink into her bed without a sound. Just the cat, waiting patiently and eagerly for her return.

A tiny sliver of happiness had been recaptured from her old life. The fear she'd felt since arriving in New Orleans began to ease. Almost allowing her to forget why she was here in the first place.

One night, Zora slid toward the back of the Petit Sapphire, clutching the sheet music she and Phillip had written the day before. The ink was still fresh and threatened to sully her bright marigold dress. The chords were still on a loop in her head.

"Baby girl Z," Miles called out from his office as she passed.

She poked her head in.

"Got somebody who wants to talk to you." Miles's deep brown forehead dripped with sweat he eagerly tried to mop away to no avail.

Zora froze, thinking of the worst possible reasons. "Who? Who wants to talk to me?"

"Come on in and find out." Miles stood behind his messy desk littered with ledgers and sheet music and ashtrays spilling over with mountains of ash. Shelves held decrepit instruments in various stages of disrepair. The walls were covered in beautiful photographs of all who had graced the club's stage. She hoped one day that hers might be among them. "You look like a baby chick scared of its own shadow," Miles said. "Be easy."

Zora inched the door open wider. There was an old white man sitting in an armchair. She flinched and took a step backward.

"Our visitor has come a long way to see you, chérie," Miles said.

Zora gazed back and forth between Miles and the strange man. Finally, the white man stood and motioned for her to sit.

Zora's eyes found Miles's, and he nodded with encouragement. "I'm supposed to get ready for my show," she said.

"*That's* precisely what I'm here to talk to you about. Are *you* the Sweet Willow of the Petit Sapphire? The young woman who sang 'Blues for Tremé' last night to a sold-out, standing-room-only crowd? The one who has crowds gathering in the street eager to hear even a strain of music slipping out the windows? Is that you?"

Zora stammered out a yes.

He reached his hand out to shake hers.

"I'm Nigel Winsome from the Lupine Jazz Group. We're based in San Francisco. We're one of the premier music companies in California, aiming to bring more of the glorious tunes west to an ever-expanding market. We also have a school. I've been scouring the country for real talent to play at our biggest venues. The kind that you have. Straight-from-the-belly singing. Natural storyteller through music. Rhythm and anticipation that can't be taught."

The way he spoke about it felt so formal. She'd never heard her music described in that way.

"We need a singer like you," he continued. "One folks remember."

"I'm not sure what you're asking," Zora said.

"I'm offering you a job. A residency."

"In San Francisco?" Zora knew nothing about that city other than what she'd read in newspapers. The hills and the trollies and the bridge that rivaled New York City's own Brooklyn Bridge. "But I have one here." She looked at Miles.

"We'd hate to lose you, but I had to make sure this man got a chance to talk to you. He said he wasn't leaving until he did." Miles lit a cigar and let out a series of smoke rings. "Couldn't even let me run him off."

"San Francisco isn't New Orleans, but it's got its own charm. Bring Sweet Willow's magic to the Bay Area. You won't regret it."

His promise of opportunity wrapped around Zora. She never thought any of this would happen. Not the sold-out performances. Not the crowds. Not the feeling of being home in a place so far away from home. She'd gotten wrapped up in her life in New Orleans now. Singing with Jo and Phillip each night and all her success in this strange, swampy city.

The thought of leaving it all behind felt exhilarating and terrifying and saddening all at once. All her options shuffled like a deck of cards before her, waiting with eager promise for her to pluck her fate from within the stack.

If she took this gig, she'd have to move even farther away from her family, across the whole country. She'd be far from Phillip and Jo, from the beautiful bright spots in her new life as Zora Broussard, not to mention Sweet Willow.

Then again, she'd made plans to give up her magic, and with it the music. In a matter of weeks, she was supposed to be in St. Louis Cemetery No. 1, ready to see Mama B. She wouldn't have a songbird voice left after that. Her ability to play any instrument she touched, gone. She might have to give up her musical relationship with Phillip, their common passion also gone.

But all this sneaking around had to end at some point. She let her mind wander back to San Francisco, a door she hadn't known existed creaking open. If she took this man up on his offer, she could keep her music, learn more about it, and perform on even bigger stages. She'd be so far from New York City and Mrs. Abernathy and all the bad things that had happened.

So long as her magic didn't do *more* bad things....

Nigel Winsome handed her a card. "Think about it. I'll be here for a couple more days. If I don't hear from you in the coming weeks, I'll figure you're staying put."

The card felt warm with promise in her palm.

A few nights later, Jo and Zora were squeezed in the backseat of Phillip's car as it darted through the French Quarter, headed for the Garden District. Miles had set them up with a house gig: singing and playing at a private party. Rocco and Phillip argued about this and that while Jo and Zora traded whispers and gossip.

Zora handed Jo a few pieces of sheet music. "Think we should sing these?"

"I don't think we'll have the acoustics for 'Heart Blues,' and I don't have no Vivi Turner kind of voice tonight. I'll need tea to do it. You'd have to take the soprano." Jo placed a newspaper cutout on top of the sheet music. A black-and-white photo of the Eiffel Tower stared back up at her. "This! This right here."

"What?"

Jo flipped the page. A big ship sat above a list of dates and times. The headline: "The Mighty Water Boulevard to Europe." "Let's convince the boys"—she nodded in their direction—"to go to Paris." Her voice tinkled like a tiny bell. "Could you imagine? Shopping on the Champs-Élysées, the croissants and tarts, performing at the clubs there, and not having to worry about colored *this* and colored *that* all the time."

Zora tried to imagine herself in the European city. The winding cobblestone streets. The long, snaking River Seine. The wonderland of lights she'd read about in the New York newspapers. It would be even farther away from home. Across an entire ocean from Mama instead of merely a train ride. The dream flickered in her chest, feeling both real and unreal.

But then she thought about Mr. Winsome and the San Francisco residency. The card tucked beneath her pillow at home; her hope that one of these nights she'd wake up from a dream and just know what decision to make.

"Admit it . . . you'd love to go." Jo's eyes brimmed with excitement.

"I would," she admitted.

"So, don't say no yet."

Zora kissed Jo's cheek. "Your dreams are as big as the Woolworth Building, you know that?"

"What's the Woolworth Building?" Jo's eyebrow hitched with confusion.

"Never mind," Zora said with a laugh. "Now, look over this music. I hope I picked the right songs for these rich white folks."

Jo burst into a fit of giggles as Phillip slowed down, looking for the right address. The houses in the Garden District had the most beautiful gas lamps that made the houses glow as if they'd trapped fireflies in glass.

"It's that one up there," Rocco said, pointing out the window.

"Look at them fancy cars all lined up. Oooo weee. Y'all are about to make some money tonight. And me too." He leapt out of the car as soon as Phillip parked.

Zora thought the gaudy cars of the rich folks looked like Fabergé eggs, and they didn't impress her. *"A whole pile of money can't cover up rot,"* her daddy would say. The garden and double porch spilled over with well-dressed people sipping drinks and eating.

"Wait here," Phillip said.

Zora and Jo lingered on the edge of the garden as Phillip and Rocco went to the front door. More party guests arrived, parking their cars and making their way through the gardens to the back. Guests slowed down as they approached Zora and Jo, curious and suspicious eyes finding them in the subtle darkness.

Jo greeted the passersby with a smile, and Zora tried her best not to scowl at whispered comments about *coloreds* and *Negroes* in the Garden District. She fussed with the beads on her dress and patted her bob to make sure not a hair was out of place. She hoped Phillip would be back as soon as possible.

"I hate coming out here," Jo said through her teeth. "These white folks think they're better than sliced bread."

"Don't white folks everywhere think that?" Zora replied.

"I reckon."

Zora elbowed Jo in her side as three white women stood on the other side of the bush opposite them, lifting long cigarette holders to their mouths.

"You think the Heinrichs will show tonight?" one asked.

The name felt familiar to Zora, but she couldn't quite place it.

"Now you oughta quit playing, Bernadette," another replied. "You know that's not that family's last name. And that woman has been holed up in that house for months now. Nobody's seen her."

"Well, *she's* the one with all the money. He should've taken her name," a third added. "But her husband doesn't seem to have the same affliction as her. On the town plenty."

"That curse came through her," the first one said. "She brings the storms. Even their block—over on Prytania—is black as night during a hot summer day."

Zora stiffened. The words of Mama B came back to her: *"I reckon the water is cursed from the Heinrich family. They brought their troubles with them."*

"My little Jean-Baptiste used to play with their son. . . . I've forgotten his name. Maybe Charles or Laurent."

"She has those grounds people out there every day trimming the Spanish moss and still no light can penetrate. I tell you. Demonic, honey. Truly the devil's work."

"How much drink have you had, Charlotte?"

Phillip peeked his head around the tall topiary bush and reached out a hand to pull Zora forward. The white women's eyes combed over her, drinking in how the edges of her dress fit snug to her hips despite her step-in undergarments, and how well the rich red of her lipstick matched her heels. "You ready, my love?" he asked.

The women gasped and fanned themselves. Zora heard all manner of grumbled curses.

Zora smiled back. "Always."

October 21, 1928

Dear Phillip,

As promised, I'm writing to let you know I am home, safe and sound. Maybe that coffin vision is wrong somehow. Or maybe it isn't me after all, someone else's red shoes. Whatever the case, I'm counting down the days until we can see each other again. I thought of a new bridge for that storm number we've been playing with. It's got a sweet little piano riff I think you might be able to handle . . . with some practice.

Love,

Zora

PS: What else do you see in your visions? What does your future hold?

October 24, 1928

Dear Zora,

Thank you. I know you think it's silly, but if I've learned anything from my family, it's to assume the worst. Somehow, though, I know if we're together and making music, all is right in the world.

Also, I bet the bridge needs an extra rest. Can't wait to try it.

Love,

Phillip

PS: I see you falling madly in love with me. But I'm already in love with you, and no mirror told me that.

13

ora couldn't keep her eyes from drooping while at the tea table with her cousins and the other debutantes from the Original Carolina Club. The late nights at Petit Sapphire and staying with Phillip until dawn were catching up with her. The days tumbled on, nearing the end of the month before she knew it. Christophe smiled at her, and she tried to chat with him, but her eyes drifted shut.

She stood in court in New York City. A white judge stared down at her, red-faced, mouth pursed in a straight line. The jury gawked at her with scowls shading their faces, and every spot on every bench in the courtroom was taken.

"Sadie Walker, you've been charged with one count of murder, five counts of bodily harm with an intention to maim, and the destruction of Eight Hundred Thirty Fifth Avenue," the judge proclaimed. "How do you plead?"

Zora gulped, turning around to look for her mama and daddy. They were bent over at the waist, crying and praying into handkerchiefs, their sniffling a low murmur.

Cameras flashed and reporters scribbled on their pads. The headlines swirled in her head:

"Daughter of Notable Musician Convicted of Murder in the First Degree"

"Charges Filed for the Murder of Abigail Marie Abernathy; Killer Sentenced to Life in Prison"

"Murderer of Oil Tycoon's Wife Found Hiding in New Orleans"

"How do you plead?" the judge asked again.

Tears rushed down her cheeks, mirroring the rain on the courtroom windows. Sweat soaked the nice white dress her mama had put her in.

"Guilty," she replied.

The court erupted. A chorus of shouts hit her one after the other like heavy rocks.

The judge cleared his throat. "I sentence you to death."

Zora's shoulder jostled. She thrashed about. Her eyes snapped open to find her aunt and the entire table of onlookers staring at her, blinking big eyes full of concern.

"Dozing at the table?" a girl named Charlotte asked, the lift of her perfect eyebrow holding disdain.

"I . . . I . . . haven't been sleeping well," Zora stammered. "I'm sorry."

Zora felt Christophe's mother's gaze on her, and she quickly looked left to avoid her. But a tiny girl named Syriah James glared back. Pink barrettes in her hair matched her dress, and Zora knew that this tea meant everything to her. The expression in her eyes reminded her of what life used to be like, when Zora was at home and excited about helping her papa with his gigs and tending to her mama's kitchen garden or wandering around Harlem playing her trumpet.

Mrs. James, the girl's mother, looked almost identical to Zora's aunt: same delicate features, neat nails, and expensive blouse. She peered at her with dreadful disdain.

"Zora," her aunt said, the sharpness of her voice erasing the nightmare. "Can I speak to you in the hall for a moment?" She flashed a smile at the others around the table as they watched with curiosity.

Zora slid out of her chair. Aunt Celine ushered her into the hall and out of earshot of the guests.

"What's going on with you, petite?" She pressed Zora's shoulders back.

"Tired is all."

"You been tired. Dragging your tail around here for months."

"I can't sleep," she fibbed. She might sleep better if she'd gotten into bed before four thirty in the morning most nights.

"Well, you need to do what you have to do." Her aunt squeezed her shoulder. "This is your chance for a good suitable marriage. It'll help you put the past in the past, where it belongs."

Part of her aunt's words rang true. It would be another way for her to start over and forget what happened back home—as much as she ever could forget about it. It would be enough of a distraction. But she had to admit it wasn't something she ever saw for herself, despite how much she honestly liked Christophe as a friend.

"I don't know if I want to get married," she said. It was only for Phillip that her heart felt open to that possibility. And they couldn't marry, could they?

"This ain't about what you want. When are you gonna realize that? It's about what you *need*." Aunt Celine pinched the bridge of her nose with exasperation. "I've talked with Dr. Bechet and his wife. We've decided you and Christophe would make an auspicious match."

"You decided?" Zora tried to keep the flare of anger out of her voice.

"Yes. And your mother and father would approve." Aunt Celine jammed her hands to her hips. "The krewe ball will be in February. We can announce the engagement then." Zora spotted tears brimming in her aunt's honey-colored eyes. "Marriage isn't all that bad. I wish every day that I had my husband back."

Part of Zora felt sad for her aunt, as wretched as she was most of the time. "I'm sorry, ma'am."

"The world is so full of struggle. You won't have that if you marry right. Speaking of which . . ." Aunt Celine leaned forward and adjusted Zora's collar, then whispered, "We've got company, sugah. Fix your face." She motioned to the left, where Christophe stood waiting.

"Yes, ma'am," she mumbled under her breath, quickly glancing at herself in the nearby wall mirror before pivoting on her heel and walking in his direction.

He grinned as if she was a kid who had just done a cartwheel in the middle of a funeral. "Are you all right?" He chuckled.

"Just tired," she admitted.

"Late nights, I suppose, Sweet Willow." He motioned his arm out for her to take it. "Walk with me?"

"Sure." Zora slipped her arm in his and let him lead her out to the hotel's beautiful topiary maze. They walked along the path in silence.

She admired the shallow ponds and their tiny fish inhabitants as well as the thick roses sharing their perfume with other folks taking in the afternoon air. But even in the fresh air, she couldn't help but yawn.

"You have to get some sleep," he said, sounding like her papa.

"Can't I sleep when I'm six feet under?" she responded.

His laugh was a deep rumble on the edge of thunder. Different from Phillip's. "I understand. I write between the hours of two a.m. and four a.m."

"You're a writer?" she asked, surprised.

"A poet . . . but you sing better than I write."

"Well, we both knew that," she teased, poking his side.

He tensed a little.

"Sorry," Zora said, peering at him. "But honestly, I have these terrible dreams." She didn't know why she even mentioned it, why she felt the need to be so honest. Maybe she wanted to make up for seeming to offend him. There was a kindness in Christophe, laced with his pride.

"Dreams about what?"

"Just things that happened before I got here." Zora felt his eyes scanning her, combing over her, as if they could find her secrets.

Christophe led her to a shaded bench. They sat and watched other colored couples mill around. Zora was grateful to be out of the heat.

"I have to tell you something, Zora," he said.

"And what is that?" she replied.

He mopped his brow. "I fancy you."

A jolt zipped up her spine.

"I would love to spend more time with you if you're willing to. I know my parents and your aunt are playing matchmaker, but for the first time, I feel like they've picked the right person." He leaned close, so close she could smell his cologne.

Before she could say a word, Christophe kissed her.

Zora avoided Phillip's gaze and touch during the entire set at the Petit Sapphire. She threw herself into the music. The excited crowd and their raucous applause and piercing whistles made her forget Christophe's sweet kiss and how confused and guilty she felt. Her aunt's wishes swirled around inside her—her wish for a gentle life for Zora, one she currently didn't have, one she knew deep down she probably could never get with Phillip, not in this city.

But she hoped the music could wash away a whole host of things.

After the set, Zora, Jo, and Phillip exited the stage to an excited crowd. For once, the music hadn't helped. She should've just canceled the show and slept. That's what her mama would've told her to do. *"You can't think right when you're dragging your feet. A good night's rest is a balm."*

Zora and Jo piled into the dressing room, wiping the sweat and makeup off, and letting the buzz of the night drain from their limbs. They changed out of their performance dresses.

"What's going on with you?" Jo asked. "You were off tonight."

"Just tired. I haven't slept."

Jo's eyes squinted with scrutiny. "It's something else. I can feel it."

Zora turned her back to Jo, not wanting her face to betray her. She was so exhausted she felt if pushed even a little, she might spill over.

Jo slipped her arms around her. "Cheer up, petite. You just need a little fun. You can sleep all day tomorrow. We're going to the late circus."

"What's the late circus?" Zora asked.

"They come every year. A white elephant shows up in the paper, and then everyone knows to stay out late for a surprise." She grabbed the *Times-Picayune* from the side table and flashed the clandestine advertisement at Zora. "Show's for the kids during the day and for adults at night. It's how they pocket more money, I suppose."

"And they let colored people in?" Zora had never been to the circus before. The ones that came through New York didn't always have a day set aside for colored people, and Papa never wanted them to try to sneak in and pay their hard-earned money to experience something other people of color couldn't. And her mother had always said Oma distrusted them, an old superstition, perhaps. Still, Zora would have been lying if she said she wasn't the least bit curious about it all. What was a circus but another place for music, performance, escape?

"Yes. For a few hours." She batted her eyes at Zora. "I don't want to miss that window . . . so c'mon . . . pretty please?"

"We just played for almost an hour. How are you not exhausted?" Zora packed away her trumpet.

"I'm all buzzy from it. You know you want to have a little fun."

"I want to lay in my bed."

"C'monnnn."

Zora rolled her eyes. Jo was irresistible when she got like this, and they both knew it. She let Jo drag her out back, where Phillip and Rocco waited with eager grins.

"Hello, gentlemen," Jo said. "We're ready."

Less than five blocks away, Zora caught sight of an evening circus at Bourbon and Toulouse Streets. The whole area was electric with movement: red-and-white striped tents, vendors offering sugary sweets, clowns throwing balls and pins, tents offering promises. The banners held a curious symbol—a crow with a two-headed snake in its mouth.

"Isn't it amazing?" Phillip said. His massive grin made him look as he must have as a child.

Red trailers passed by first, and each one advertised its contents: roaring lions and tigers, charging rhinos and furious hippos, and a majestic white elephant at the very end. The animals peeked out from their cages. Zora felt the energy radiating through the cobblestones beneath her. A brass band's melody escaped the great tent, and smells of hand-spun candy and fresh popcorn met her nose.

Zora heard feline roars and the trumpet blare of an elephant's trunk. White trailers came next, carrying men and women in sequined outfits and feather headdresses. They jumped from trailer windows like monkeys and performed acrobatic jumps and somersaults and flip-tricks across the procession's rooftops.

The last set of vehicles chugged around the street's perimeter. Each car slid open for a quick peek inside a black frame: a plump lady and her plump daughter on a bed of enormous pillows; a man covered with hair from head to toe; a group of tiny people no bigger than Zora's leg, eating tea and biscuits; and a veiled woman gazing into a crystal ball. Zora could see the sign on her table read "Madame Saule's Solarium of Secrets." She felt like she could watch the demonstration like a moving picture forever.

Saule. She said the word aloud, stumbling over its pronunciation.

Phillip repeated it in French. "It means 'willow,' curiously enough."

Two men marched out, climbed on striped platforms, and hollered into megaphones. Their voices echoed above the noise of the crowd, and Zora felt each booming word in her chest. Everything felt exaggerated and stretched, and Zora didn't know if it was because she was so exhausted or if it was because of the guilt she felt. She knew she should tell Phillip about the kiss with Christophe and about her aunt's plans for their future. But each time the words bubbled up, they made her feel sick.

"You like it?" Phillip asked.

All manner of people walked through the makeshift tents. She'd never seen men of different skin colors occupy the same space. New York City was not a city that always kept mixed company. The New York Zora knew was carefully sorted, just like its many boroughs and neighborhoods. She still wondered if the scene taking place before her was normal in a port city like New Orleans, one where people from all over the world congregated and descended upon. She'd found the color line both firm in some places and loose in others.

"Hey . . ." Phillip searched her face. "Are you okay?"

She answered him with a weak smile. She wished she could grab his hand, that they could anchor themselves to each other and walk forward.

The barkers took turns yelling into their megaphones about the circus amusements: Clown Alley, moving panoramas, historical pageants, aerialists, gymnasts of the world, a Noah-like menagerie and sideshow, and the last great oracle of the world, hailing from across the globe. At the center of the hubbub they unfurled a banner. Great, curly words burst across it and announced: "The Müller Brothers Traveling Circus has come to play. Will you join?"

Rocco and Jo abandoned them, heading to the menagerie. Zora called after her, but her voice was swallowed in the crowd's excitement.

"Ha, would you look at that? What a lark." Phillip pointed at a nearby poster that said "Fortune-Teller This Way." "Want to discover the future with me?"

"Okay," she replied, following behind him with curiosity and trepidation. Who was to say this person didn't actually have powers like Phillip and her? What if the fortune-teller revealed that she would have to marry Christophe—or that she even considered it? What if she and Phillip were told that they would never be together? What if they heard something that would leave cracks in the newness of their relationship? There was so much she hadn't told him—her plans with Mama B, the residency in San Francisco. What if the fortune-teller told Phillip how unsure she was about everything right now?

Lampposts lit the way through the dark corridors. The future felt terrifying with each step they took through the crowds. The moonlight couldn't penetrate the deep dark of the sideshow area, and one who wandered through the passageways might lose track of the hour, tricked into believing it was still the early evening as the hours inched toward midnight and into the morning. They weaved through the black tents, cutting through more groups of people waiting to file into the exhibits. Colors blurred in the corners of Zora's eyes. Bodies moved in slow motion around her. She felt trapped underwater.

The signage sprouted in rapid succession like tiny mushrooms popping up in a row. They pointed her down a darker path where there was no lamppost. A frayed tent blocked the end of the path. It was the color of white ash and stood out from the other tents around it.

Phillip glanced back at her. "Ready?"

"I guess."

"What does that mean? What's wrong?"

She didn't know how to tell him. She didn't want to ruin the night. "Nothing. I'm all right."

He looked left and right, then took her hand and kissed it.

They ducked inside.

It was empty except for a large covered box in the center. Zora and Phillip moved closer, one step at time. She could spot rich colors under the heavy cloth—red, black, white, and gold—glittering like candies in a box. Zora's fingers grazed the velvet drape, and she had a feeling that she shouldn't touch it. But she slid it back anyway.

The gilded box held a life-size woman's form, encased in glass. The figure appeared from the waist up, as if it were seated at a table, and it was hunched over a cloudy crystal ball that sat in a golden holder like an enormous pearl. The woman's face looked like it might crumble at the slightest touch, and she wore a veil littered with moth-eaten holes. Her head was bowed, her eyes closed, and her lips pursed.

Zora didn't know if the woman was real or not, if it was a machine or a joke. Inside the glass stood a placard.

YOUR FORTUNE AWAITS!

LET THE POWERFUL MADAME SAULE FORECAST YOUR FUTURE.

DROP A DIME IN THE SLOT. LOOK INTO HER CRYSTAL BALL.

SEE WHAT'S IN STORE!

"Maybe we should put a coin in and see what happens?" Phillip pulled a dime from his pocket and reached for the slot.

A card dropped into a small compartment before he could put it inside. A light illuminated a tiny door handle. Zora tugged the knob, then reached in for the card. The woman's eyes snapped open, and she grabbed Zora's wrist.

Zora shrieked. A wrinkled white face stared back. The eyes, now open, were hollow. Her nails sank deep into Zora's hand. "They're looking for you, and they will find you," she said.

The woman tightened her grip. Zora tried to pull her hand free.

"They all will come. Give up your magic now."

Phillip began to shout. "Is this is a joke?"

The woman leaned close to the glass. "Beware of magic and mirrors and misfortune," she hissed. "The crow and the snake will be fed!"

Zora's stomach flip-flopped. The woman clucked her tongue and loosened her grip, and Zora stumbled backward.

"I don't understand," Zora said, feeling the room turning around her. Her arm ached. Her head pounded.

"Magic has consequences, children. You must relinquish it before you pay with blood."

And then, behind the glass, the woman disappeared in pieces: first her hands and arms, then her torso, and last, her face, blowing away like bits of shredded newspaper.

14

Three days passed slowly, like grains of sand falling in an hourglass. The house swelled with folks from the Original Carolina Club, and her aunt worked hard to impress them, forcing Zora and her cousins to help her spoil and host. Zora fumbled with the tea sets and dropped beignets and mixed up the overly perfumed ladies' names. She couldn't seem to say the right thing at the right time, because her mind was occupied with the woman's message: *"Beware of magic and mirrors and misfortune. The crow and the snake will be fed!"*

The words were the last she thought of as she drifted off to sleep and the first thing on her mind when she woke in the morning. Zora still felt shaky about it all.

The night before Halloween, her fingers trembled as she slipped on her red shoes and sneaked out of the house to meet Phillip. He'd been as rattled as she was after the circus, believing that the words that predicted some awful future would come true. He'd wanted to stand outside her house all night to make sure she was safe, until she convinced him that there would be more trouble for both of them if he was discovered.

But now that the days had added up, she needed to see him. They needed to talk about what happened at the circus, about his visions, about whatever the crow and snake were, and if they were in danger.

Phillip waited for her in Jackson Square, a big smile lighting up his face. Her hand found his, now a reflex, as she blinked up at him in surprise. "How are you so calm after what happened?"

"I'm not calm. I have a plan, and this is part of it." He led her left and right, and down this street and that street, until he stopped abruptly at a corner.

"Where are we?"

"You'll see. But first..." He put his warm palms over her eyes briefly, tugging her toward a nearby building. "Don't open them," he whispered.

Zora tried to clamp her eyes shut, but her eyelids fought to stay open. She desperately wanted to see where they were going. "Where are you taking me?"

"You'll see." His words hit the nape of her neck, leaving a tingle behind.

When Rocco had brought her Phillip's latest letter, she'd figured they would walk to the club. But he was leading her forward and into what felt like an enclosed space. A closet? An elevator? Zora took a deep sniff, but all she could smell was fresh paint and dust. She tried not to get irritated. "Phillip, we *need* to talk. This is no time for games," she said. Her eyelids snapped open. They were in a shoddy-looking elevator.

"Eyes closed," Phillip replied. "This is *no* game."

"I don't take orders from you," she said with a smile.

"That much I do know. One more minute."

"Fine, fine, fine." She steeled her shoulders and stretched up. She closed her eyes again.

She heard the elevator doors open, and Phillip led Zora out. The warmth of the night settled over her skin, the scents of New Orleans tickled her nose, and she heard jazz.

"Three, two, one . . . Open," he said.

They were on a rooftop overlooking the French Quarter. Below, Zora looked at the beautiful St. Louis Cathedral and spotted bowler hats and cloches and people pouring in and out of jazz bars. Bundles of crimson roses surrounded a blanket laid out at her feet. "Phillip..."

He took her hand and pulled her forward.

Zora's red shoes remained glued in place. "Is this all for me?"

"Who else?"

The question felt silly.

"I wanted to show you how much I cared. This isn't just about magic and visions and bad luck. It's about us—you and me. It's about how not a lot of things in my life have made sense. But you do. You make sense to me."

"I just..." The words were gone again. "Where are we?"

"One of the buildings my father owns." He sat on the blanket.

"Your father owns buildings, too?" How different were their backgrounds?

She sat next to him, and then they lay down, side by side, arms and legs tangled up, gazing up at the full moon and listening to the music escaping the street. Phillip tapped the rhythm on her thigh. It sent a pulse racing through her.

"What are we going to do?"

"Fall in love," he replied, lifting her wrist to his mouth.

"Phillip, I'm serious."

"I am, too," he replied.

"I'm scared."

He kissed her worries back into her, then pointed up at the moon. "My mother used to tell me that God fashioned the moon after his lover."

"God had a lover?"

"I think so. How could he have known what beautiful things to make if he didn't?" He gave her hand a squeeze. "She said his love was his peace. That's why the moon is so calming and tranquil. That it was love at first sight." He nuzzled his face into the crook of her neck. "That's how I feel about you. I knew from the moment I heard your voice that I never wanted to hear another."

She bit her bottom lip and turned to gaze into his blue eyes. How had he not been afraid? How had he so easily loved her when there were so many obstacles between them? How did he silence all the warnings of danger?

"Was it not like that for you?" A flicker of doubt appeared in his eyes.

"I was afraid. I am still afraid," she said. "All the things that have happened..."

"So you didn't fancy me when we first met?" He pressed his hand to his chest in mock upset.

"You were dangerous. You *are* dangerous." The safe choice of Christophe appeared in her head.

He smiled.

Frustration burst inside her, and she sat up.

She took a deep breath. "Loving you has consequences. Real-life ones—not just some coffin in a mirror. We could both go to jail. We could be hurt. White people don't want to share bus seats with colored folks, let alone see us together." An upset rose in her throat. "Have you seen the papers? Two black men were strung up in St. Tammany Parish three weeks ago because someone accused them of looking at a white woman. Last month, three children were taken from the Bertrand home because a colored woman was living with the white father of her children. The world can hurt us. The world can hurt *me* for loving you. So no, I didn't see you and think, *I love you just by looking at you.*"

Phillip's breathing slowed, and he didn't say anything for a long minute. "I'm sorry. I just didn't think ... I just didn't know ... or realize."

Zora kissed him, trying to send a message through her lips. "I loved your music first."

His blond eyebrows lifted. "My music?"

"The first time I heard you play. That's when I knew."

The different melodies from the clubs below ebbed and flowed, mixing into a new song just for them.

He stood and reached for her. "Dance with me."

Phillip took Zora's hand and helped her up. She folded into his body, wrapped in the salty sweet of his smell. They rocked and swayed to the music escaping the street. Her eyes closed, and she let him move her left and right. She thought of how different it was to dance with him like this.

"I was raised in a house where no one even yelled," he whispered in her ear. "There was no emotion. I laugh and joke because I don't know how else to be." His heart thudded so hard she felt it vibrate through her. "I'm terrified of losing you. Of anything happening to you."

Zora placed a hand on his cheek and looked up. "But I'm still here."

He shook his head. "I see your shoes in every damn reflection."

"Then show me." She paused. "Show me the image. How does it work?"

Phillip took a deep breath. He went to the blanket and set aside the wine, grabbing a carafe of water. "Cup your hands together. Don't let them break. I need a still surface."

Zora nodded. He filled her palms with water, a small vessel, then closed his eyes and took a deep breath.

Zora watched his pale white cheeks flush as he concentrated. The moonlight danced across the water in her hands, then stretched into a warm sphere of light. A shrouded coffin appeared, its edges sharp. Inside, the body was obscured. But there at the bottom, peeking through the glass, were red shoes, like a bloodstain. From one angle, they were the delicate slippers with ribbons, but as Zora shifted her head, she could see the transformation glimmering through—the small heel, the T-strap. There was no mistaking them. They were her shoes.

Zora gasped and dropped the water.

"That's what I see. It's why I'm worried if you're a minute late to the Petit Sapphire or if I don't get a letter from you. I'm panicked."

"But I'm fine," she assured him.

"Leave New Orleans with me. We can elope. We can go away where none of this follows us. There are places where colored and white people marry and live in peace. You can still sing and I can play the piano. We can be together. *Truly* together."

She looked up at him, desperate to believe in him. "But how?"

"As long as we're together, we'll be safe. That image won't come true. We won't let it."

Their eyes locked. He lifted a box from his pocket and opened it. A glittering diamond shone back at her.

She gasped. He had been thinking about this for a while. Enough time to get a ring. Phillip kissed her. "Dance with me forever. Play music with me forever."

She closed her eyes and thought for one long moment. Could she dance with him forever even if she didn't know what rhythm or refrain would come next? Would they be able to face whatever the world threw at them? If she got rid of her magic tomorrow, maybe she could bargain with Mama B to leave behind her music. To break the rules of magic just a little. Maybe she could find a way to have everything—to keep Phillip safe from her magic and also make music with him.

"Wait," she replied, dropping her hand into her pocket to pull out Mr. Winsome's card, showing Phillip the smooth raised calligraphy. "What about San Francisco?" She told him about the job offer.

His eyes brightened. "Yes. This is perfect. We can take the train."

"We'd have to travel in separate cars," she reminded him.

"It'll be the last time," he said. "And I'll be waiting to kiss you on the platform when we get there."

She took a deep breath, bracing herself.

"Yes," she said before her head could talk her out of it. "Yes, I'll marry you."

Phillip twirled her, then pulled her in for a kiss.

15

ora sat in the window with her cat, watching a dark storm roll in. She figured it was fitting. Halloween night should be terrifying, after all. She gazed into the jar Mama B had given her. How would Mama B's roots and magic take away her own? What had such power? Would any of this actually work? Why had she ever believed heeding the terrifying fortune-teller's warning was a good plan?

Phillip had told her about other visions he'd had besides the coffin one—terrible storms and loud gunshots and more bad luck. But like the bad dreams she often had, the magic inside her was decidedly worse. It had consequences. Grave ones. Getting rid of it would be best.

She'd rehearsed telling Phillip about Mrs. Abernathy, hoping that the way he looked at her didn't harden and change once he discovered the worst things she'd ever done. She'd tell him it was all behind her now. Yes, they'd leave, but she didn't want any of this catching up to them on the road. She didn't want to lose her temper ever again and have another outburst that they'd have to run from.

The streets were filled with partygoers in costume. She'd feigned stomach cramps to stay behind from the krewe celebrations her aunt and cousins were attending. Zora put on the red shoes, pressing her toes into the grooves, the imprints left behind by her oma, her mama, and who knows what other ancestors. Her heart squeezed. This would be the last time she'd be wearing them.

She pushed away thoughts of her mother's reaction. She was doing the right thing. This was the best chance for her future. And hopefully there would be a way to keep the music—at least some of it. She could give up the instruments, maybe, if she still had her voice.

The cat nuzzled his head into her hand and nipped at her dress, tugging it with his teeth. She figured if he could talk, he would probably try to convince her not to do what she was about to do.

"What would *you* do?" she asked him.

She waited for the cat to answer her.

He meowed.

"I wish you could tell me. I wish we could find out if this whole thing would work."

The house was so empty, the sound of the room's clock ticking made her feel each and every minute until it struck 11:00 p.m.

"Time to go," she said to the cat, rubbing his ginger head.

With each step she took closer to the graveyard, Zora's arms and legs trembled. She took a deep breath, clutching the jar tight to her chest. Her pulse drummed. She'd said she was going to do it; she'd made a decision. This was for the best.

Couples passed by, holding hands or cuddling. She hoped one day she could just be walking with Phillip and talking about all the silly things either of them had seen during their day, not worrying about coffins and magic and visions.

At the graveyard entrance stood Mama B. Swaddled in white, she held a long carved staff. In the parade of mourners, she didn't stand out. "You looking like a scared baby chick, honey," she clucked at Zora. "Magic has no room for fear." She turned and walked ahead into the graveyard, then turned back. "You coming?"

Zora moved forward.

A sea of crypts and mausoleums spread out before them. In New Orleans on Halloween, graveyards were busy. Mourners decorated them with flowers and candles. Some left food. Some arranged to have their pictures taken. Zora could never get used to the dead sprinkled about aboveground, outside their proper resting place caged in the earth.

Zora didn't know if she was strong enough to stop shaking. "Could you take away just pieces of the magic? The parts that get me in trouble? Is there a way to keep the music? Or some of it at least?"

Mama B spun around on her tiny heel. "We've been over this. It's all or *nothing*. You want nothing?"

Zora clamped her eyes shut, and she thought of San Francisco. What was it the fortune-teller at the circus had said? *"You must relinquish it before you pay with blood."* Zora had done terrible things, and more were yet to come if she kept the magic in her veins. She could even hurt Phillip. If she lost the music, maybe she could teach herself again. People did it all the time without magic. Phillip could play music in her stead as she relearned.

Zora nodded. "Okay. I'll do it."

"For the full bargain."

"Yes, ma'am."

Zora followed behind Mama B as she stopped at the very edge of the graveyard in what felt like the darkest corner.

Mama B raised her staff in the air. A soft light trickled from the very tip of the wood, spreading out and descending upon them like a quilt stitched with starlight. "This'll keep any nosy folks out of our business," she explained. She reached for Zora's jar and inspected it. "I took some of those nightmares from you. Not all of them. There were so many. But this jar is charged with your spirit now."

"What's going to happen?" Zora asked, trying to hide the tremble in her voice.

Mama B glanced up. "Don't put the jar down until I tell you," she said. "And hold tight."

Zora gripped the mason jar between her hands. The cool glass heated. Wind rushed inside the pocket Mama B had made. Lightning bolts danced along the crypts, teasing the stone with their heat.

She braced herself.

Snowflakes fell like feathers from heaven. Thunder roared. The fine hairs on her arms stood up, warning of an imminent strike.

"Set it down now," Mama B yelled.

Zora put the jar at her feet and scrambled back.

The lid flipped open. She could feel her hair escaping its bun, becoming a halo of billowing curls. The sphere of electricity sizzled. A blinding light filled the space. Mama B's cloak worked. Right beside them, two little boys visited the grave of their grandfather and didn't even turn to look.

Then the air filled with a creaky, stretching sound. From within the jar, willow bark grew into long braids, twisting and twirling until they were long ropes. They coiled together into a wreath, then a large trellis bursting with snow-white flowers. A wooden door etched with a symbol appeared.

A willow tree.

She looked back at Mama B. "What do I do?"

"It's a door, child," Mama B said. "Open it."

"Where does it go?"

"The time for questions is over." Mama B swatted at her.

As she reached for the doorknob, Zora braced herself for the pain and the price of getting rid of her gift.

It shot open.

"Enkelin," a voice called out.

Her eyes snapped open.

It was her oma.

16

athilda stood in the doorway, wizened and beautifully wrinkled, her silver-and-white hair gathered into a bun. Bright and familiar eyes stared back at Zora.

"Oma?"

"Yes, yes, it's me."

Zora ran straight into her arms and folded herself into her grandmother's warmth. She smelled the same—like lavender and soap—and she felt the same—like bread fresh from the oven. Tears streamed down Zora's face, a deep guttural cry escaping her.

"What are you doing here?" she asked.

"You called me."

Zora looked back at Mama B.

"If you want to get rid of your magic, then you must give it back to those who gave it to you," Mama B replied smugly. "I told you this required the ancestors, Zora."

Oma's eyebrows lifted. "Liebling? My Sadie."

The sound of Zora's real name brought tears to her eyes. Oma fingered Zora's hair and gazed at her. How would she explain it all? What would she think? How disappointed would she be?

"Get rid of your magic? The gifts I gave you? And the ones from your other grandmother?"

The door opened again, and out strode a beautiful older woman in the most decadent church hat. Apple-shaped and casket sharp, she stomped forward as if she owned the land beneath her feet. The moonlight made the deep browns in her skin almost glow.

Her grandma Queenie. Her papa's mother.

She'd seen one picture of her.

Queenie marched right up to them. "What's all this trouble, Mathilda?"

Oma introduced them. Zora felt like looking into her grandma Queenie's eyes was like staring into her papa's, and she instantly filled with sadness, missing her parents.

"I was sorry not to have been there." The warmth in her voice mingled with the warmth of Oma's hand on her shoulder. The combination of it slowed Zora's heart and she felt like maybe...maybe... she could get it all out.

"Now, spit it out, sugah. What's going on?" Queenie asked.

The story tumbled out of Zora piece by piece. She tried hard not to cry as she told them about Mrs. Abernathy and Mama and the burns and how the building came crashing down and the sounds of the screams. Then she told them what happened when she tried to protect Jo at the Orleans Roof Garden and how her magic seemed uncontrollable.

Oma put a hand to her mouth as Zora finished. Queenie paced in circles, muttering "Lord have mercy" over and over. "I left too soon, before I could show you how to use it. Why didn't your mama instruct you?"

"Without you around, she forbade magic in the house. It was too hard for her." Zora dropped to her knees in front of her grandmothers. "I need you to take it away. I can't control it. I don't even know how it truly works."

Queenie and Mathilda looked at each other, then helped Zora to stand up.

"If we take it, you won't be protected. This magic has been gifted to you because you come from a long line of wielders on both sides. It's carried in the blood and the marrow, sweetheart." Queenie patted Zora's shoulder.

Oma took her hand and kissed it. "Promises have power. Your gifts are our promise to you. To keep you safe. Darkness is coming."

Queenie took off her church hat and tapped it. The base filled with water. "Come look and see what's to come."

They all gazed in.

Flash after flash, images came quick as a moving picture show. Visions of people Zora had never seen: a young man who resembled Phillip in an odd short-brimmed hat next to a well; candlelight flickering across the frightened face of a beautiful light brown girl; and a boy and girl in strange, colorful clothing, running past tall skyscrapers.

In her heart, she felt like she knew them all.

"They're the line. Our line," Queenie said. "If we were to take your magic, none of this could come to pass. Our family would come to an end with you."

"Disrupting time always leads to bad things," Oma warned, pursing her thin lips. "Now, where is your mama?"

"Back in New York. She veiled me so no one could find me after what happened."

Oma's eyes lit up. "Did I teach you anything?" She threw her wrinkled hands in the air.

"Mama's trying to hide what I did. She thinks if she does that, I'll be able to come home soon."

Oma started to curse in German.

"Mathilda, what are we going to do about this mess?" Queenie asked.

Zora's heart knocked around in her chest. "Please. If you take the magic, then I won't make any more mistakes. There's someone after me for it. I was told, at the circus—"

"What did I always say about circuses?" Oma scolded. "They're dangerous."

"Please, Oma, please, I beg you…take it." Tears flooded Zora's cheeks like the rain above.

A person stepped through Mama B's shroud and shouted, "Don't do it!"

All of them whipped around.

Phillip stood there, holding an ornate mirror.

17

"What are you doing here?" Zora asked him.

"More importantly, how did you see past my veil?"
Mama B pointed her staff at him, the tip now pointed and sharp.
"We're in a graveyard, so it'll be easy to dispose of you. Don't test
me, boy."

"The mirror. That's how I knew to come. I saw Zora upset. I saw
the graves. I thought she was in danger." Phillip's cheeks were red as
tomatoes.

"Where did you get that mirror?" Oma stepped forward. Phillip let her touch the mirror. "This is one of mine. I made a pair a long time ago. From the same sheet of glass."

"It's a family heirloom," Phillip said.

She spoke to him in German, and he responded fluently.

"It couldn't be," Oma said with a gasp. There was a loud crack.

Mama B put her staff in the air. "The magic is waning. It'll be dawn soon. A decision must be made."

Zora took Oma's hand. "Whose mirror is this? What does this all mean?"

"This young man is the descendant of someone I used to know. Someone I used to care about," Oma replied. "That mirror belonged to her."

Queenie gazed into her hat again. "They've kissed." Oma's eyes grew big with worry, and her gaze volleyed between Phillip and Zora. "Your love brought them together," Queenie added, looking at Oma.

Oma took Zora's chin and lifted it. Her light brown eyes bored into Zora's. "And *you* already love *him*. I can feel it in your spirit."

The top of the door behind them crashed to the ground.

"The veil is waning. You have to go," Mama B shouted.

Queenie extended her brown hands to Zora, and she took them. "You're stronger than you know. You need to keep your magic safely where we put it. Down in the bones where it belongs." Queenie patted her on the back, kissed her cheek, then adjusted her hat before placing it perfectly back on her head. "Let's go, Mathilda. I'm not cut out to haunt."

Oma pulled Zora into a hug, and Zora begged her to stay.

"I can't take it, liebling. Queenie is right." She pulled back with eyes full of tears and placed a hand on Zora's cheek. "You will need your gifts for the days ahead." Her eyes cut to Phillip. "Be careful with my mirror—and my most precious love."

The spirits of Queenie and Mathilda faded into the door. The frame began to smolder and illuminate the night. They stood in silence as the glittering net above them tapered off, drifting out into the distance. The last bit of wind zipped through, and the crystalline tones of the jar sounded.

Mama B approached it and tipped it over. "Well, wasn't that something?"

Zora crouched down and cried. Phillip knelt beside her and rubbed her back, but she couldn't stop. The tears flew out of her despite her embarrassment.

The magic still hummed inside her.

"Don't mean to interrupt this love nest, sugahs, but I'll be needing my payment. Those shoes."

Zora stood, her bones cracking and aching from the long night. "But I still have my magic."

"That was you and your grandmothers' decision. Doesn't mean I am not supposed to get paid." She huffed, stamping her staff on the ground.

Phillip took out his wallet and handed her a sheaf of bills. "For your trouble."

"It was more than trouble, young man. It was a lot of work. Closed up my shop for the night. One of the best nights of the year, fooling with her." She pointed at Zora's feet. "I was promised those."

"I can't. They're all I have left of my oma now," Zora replied.

"You have her magic running through your veins still." She jammed a hand to her hip. "And that's not my problem."

Phillip held the bills firm in his hand.

"A promise is a promise. A contract is a contract." Mama B scowled and snatched the money. "Mark my words. You've swallowed a storm of misfortune. It will drown you before long. You thought your family was bad luck before..."

Mama B stomped off. Zora held her breath until the old woman disappeared from view.

"I'll pay you back," Zora mumbled.

"You won't have to," he answered.

Mama B's words still burned. Another thing Zora wondered might break her and Phillip.

18

hillip held Zora's hand the entire walk home. People stared. People grumbled. Even though their palms sweated, he didn't let go.

Zora still couldn't stop shaking. She'd seen her oma. She'd seen her grandmother Queenie. She'd almost given up her magic. The details of the night were like a record player skipping and jumping and scratching. She opened her mouth to talk about it, to try to make sense of it all. A sob escaped.

Phillip shushed her. "It's going to be all right. We're going to be all right. I won't let anything happen to you."

"I thought by getting rid of my magic, I would be able to live this brand-new life," she said. "Away from Mrs. Abernathy and all the things that happened back home." Her shoulders tightened.

"Who is Mrs. Abernathy? What happened in New York?"

"She's the reason I wanted to get rid of my magic." Zora took a deep breath. The story tumbled out in waves. Embarrassment and shame set into her cheeks, and she felt like she'd swallowed the sun.

He nodded as if she'd merely said she grew up in a brownstone in Harlem and ate chicken pot pies for dinner. He didn't flinch at the sound of it all.

Phillip took her hand again. "You were protecting your mother. I would've done the same . . . and that's what you did for Jo that night at the Orleans Roof Garden, too."

"I was born with it," she admitted. "I've always been able to move things with my will. My desires pouring out of me like music notes, taking things from one place to another. Before my grandmother died, she would help me control it, but she didn't get a chance to teach me enough."

"And your mother?"

"She could pour her will into the things she cooked or baked. Influencing people's emotions with a simple piece of sweet potato pie."

"I know a lot about secrets and magic, you know that." He took out the strange mirror again and showed it to her. She held the beautiful object in her hands, tracing along its gilded edges and wondering how Oma made such a beautiful thing and what kind of power it possessed, what secrets it was hiding.

"I wish you'd trusted me enough to tell me before..." he said.

"I don't know much about my magic. Mama forbade me from using it after Oma died. I didn't know that it would come out of me like that when I got upset. I just didn't know."

"Then we'll face it all together. I will keep you safe *and* you will keep me safe." He lifted Zora's hand. "There's a lot of power in these beautiful hands. I'd never want to cross a beautiful woman such as yourself...or ever stand in your way."

Zora tried to let his confidence soak into her. She hugged him before turning to go.

"I'm going to walk you to the door tonight," he said.

"You shouldn't," she replied.

"It would make me feel better. To see that you got inside. Please."

Zora looked up at him, and his face told her that there was no use in arguing.

They walked the long route through the French Quarter to the back-a-town. She leaned into him, her limbs heavy with exhaustion, and hoped that by the time they reached her aunt's house, her heart would find its regular rhythm.

A police car sped down the block, then stopped and reversed. Its headlights were blinding.

Phillip put his hand up to block the light. Zora stiffened and pulled Phillip's jacket tight around her.

The policeman rolled his window down. "What are you doing out so late?" he asked Phillip, his eyes finding Zora.

"It's a nice night," Phillip answered.

The policeman leaned out the window and nodded at Zora. "Soliciting is up to five years in jail, you know? This ain't Storyville no more."

Zora's jaw clenched, and her fists balled.

"This lovely lady is not soliciting. I wanted to make sure she got home safely. Have a great night, sir." Phillip wrapped an arm around Zora.

The policeman gave them a threatening look.

Zora held her breath. He could arrest them right here and right now. He could beat them both. Or worse. And no one could do anything about it.

The policeman spat chewing tobacco at their feet before driving down the street.

Zora's stomach was filled with bile, but she couldn't say a word as they reached her aunt's house.

Phillip put a hand on her tense shoulder. "That was awful. I know—"

The door swung open. Aunt Celine's frame filled the doorway. "Do you have any idea what time it is?" Zora flinched as she tromped down the back stairs. She snatched Zora by the arm and yanked her away from Phillip.

"And who is this?" Aunt Celine craned to inspect Phillip in the dark. "You running around with this boy?"

Phillip stepped forward and began to introduce himself. Celine swatted away his words as if they were flies trying to get into the house.

"I have no interest in who you might be. Whatever this is, it ends *tonight*. You hear me?"

Phillip's cheeks flamed, and his eyes cut to Zora.

"Won't be any explaining or talking. Almost-engaged girls don't stay out late. Almost-engaged girls don't pal around with men who aren't their future betrothed. Almost-engaged colored girls most definitely don't mix with white men. You could've been jailed or ... worse."

"*We're* engaged," Zora blurted out.

Aunt Celine's cheeks shook with anger. "The law wouldn't even allow you to."

"But—" Zora started to protest, but Aunt Celine marched her up the stairs and slammed the door behind her. Zora didn't even get a chance to look back.

Aunt Celine whipped around to face Zora. "You will never see him again."

"But, Aunt Celine—"

"You will accept an offer of marriage from Christophe Bechet Jr. Your mama and daddy have already sent their blessing and money to help with the wedding expenses. It's done. And don't think I'm letting you out of my sight. Into my dressing studio. You'll sleep there for now."

Aunt Celine locked her inside.

Zora curled up on the tiny cot bed in the corner and cried herself to sleep.

November 10, 1928

Dearest Phillip,

Please forgive me. Please trust that I love you. Please know that I don't want to be with anyone but you.

I didn't think to tell you about Christophe because I never planned to ever accept his marriage proposal. I accepted yours, and I plan to keep it.

I wrote to Mr. Winsome, accepting his offer and telling him that I would be bringing my pianist and husband. I await his letter. I'll send word as soon as I have it.

But my aunt Celine won't let me leave the house. Threatened Ana, Evelyn, and even Mabel with dire consequences if they let me leave. Rocco promised to give this to you after he dropped off my aunt's weekly libations. It seems the krewe party season is in full swing.

I miss you.

Love,

Zora

November 18, 1928

    Dearest love,

    I could never be upset with you.

    I just wish I could come take you from that house. I drive by it every day looking for a glimpse of you, needing to see your face and know that you are all right. I am figuring out a plan. Rocco will continue to carry the letters, and he will help you leave when the time is right.

    And as soon as you hear from Mr. Winsome in San Francisco, I'll buy our tickets.

    We will be together soon.

    Love,

    Phillip

December 4, 1928

 Dearest Phillip,

 My aunt has been making me meet with Christophe Bechet Jr. once a week for tea. I cannot bear it much longer. She's made my wedding dress. I have to look at it on the dress form every night from my cot. It's a beautiful simple gown that I couldn't bear to have to wear without you waiting to see me in it. She and Christophe's mother have been planning the details of the engagement.

 I miss our music. I miss our nightly performances. How is Jo doing at singing our songs? I tried to see if she would be allowed to visit me, but my aunt won't entertain any of it. I'm still a trapped mouse in her room.

 There's still been no letter from Mr. Winsome. Mabel checks the post for me every day.

 What are we going to do?

 Love,

 Zora

December 26, 1928

Dearest love,

Christmas was horrible without you. I'm sorry I wasn't able to write you a letter sooner. My mother had another bad spell, and Rocco got sent away by his uncle for several weeks on a task. Miles postponed your shows because your fans have been upset that Jo has been taking your place. She has a beautiful voice but is no you. She's not Sweet Willow, and Miles is tired of dealing with upset customers demanding their money back. I told him that you've been very ill and without the use of your voice. We will figure out what to do about our show once you're free of your aunt's house.

I've ironed out all the details of the plan. Rocco has found a priest who will marry us in a small chapel just outside of New Orleans in St. Charles Parish. He has another package scheduled to deliver to your aunt on February 5. The night of the Carolina Krewe ball. Be packed and prepared to leave at midnight.

We will be together soon.

The hours feel like millennia.

Love,

Phillip

19

The January skies held big fluffy clouds without a hint of rain. Aunt Celine hustled Zora, Ana, and Evelyn out of the house, wanting to arrive early to the Magnolia Hotel for the krewe ball rehearsal so they could scope out who might actually be the contenders for krewe queen.

This was the first time that Zora had been let out of the house. She inhaled a breath of fresh air before they squeezed into the backseat of the car her aunt had hired.

"Hush up and pay attention!" Aunt Celine swatted at their legs until they settled down.

Zora gazed out the window, taking in the city as it prepared for Mardi Gras: garlands being hung from storefronts, the scent of sweets in the air, people carrying pieces of parade floats and large signs, shop-keepers painting windows in festive colors.

"Hurry! Hurry!" Aunt Celine said to the driver as if they were in a horse-drawn carriage and off to court.

Ana and Evelyn argued back and forth about the white women debutantes who would be in the *Times-Picayune* and how Evelyn had won twenty-five cents guessing which one would win. "It's always the ones with heart-shaped faces, I tell you," Evelyn proclaimed. "Those are the ones anointed Queen of Mardi Gras."

The hired car sailed into the hotel parking lot. Aunt Celine foisted a few coins into the colored driver's hands. Zora spotted Christophe and his brothers with their mother. His large palm swallowed her manicured hand as he gallantly led her in. Before Zora had met Phillip, she never wished anyone would hold her hand like that, wanting it to be free to feel the air lacing between her fingertips or ready to feel the cool brass of her trumpet keys. But now, as she gazed down at her palm, she missed the warmth of Phillip's hand, wished he were there to cut her nerves over all this debutante mess.

"Let's go," Aunt Celine said. "I want to catch up with Mrs. Bechet. Make sure she still plans on hiring me to sew her gown; we're practically family at this point. Hurry on now!"

Elegant white bricks and twinkling lights made the Magnolia Hotel look like a Renaissance castle. Ana and Evelyn whispered to each other, trading gossip and secrets about every girl who passed. Clusters of kids cluttered the room. Chatting voices boomed all around like pockets of sound. The faces of the other kids in the room were a blur of brown. Men in uniforms decorated the room's white walls. Golden drapes dropped down in front of high windows, and tables were rolled in.

Zora ducked behind her cousins. Aunt Celine left them, headed off to mingle with the other mothers in the back of the room at tables dotted with coffee- and teapots. Looking around for a familiar face, Zora wished Jo came from a different type of family. If she were here, she would've tried to get Zora to escape to the bathroom just before the rehearsal dance started. They'd fall onto the couches in there and laugh, imagining everyone looking for them, two ships out to sea.

Christophe Bechet Jr. made his way over to her. Ana squirmed, primping and adjusting herself. Her aunt had sung his praises in the car, trying to prime at least one of them to make sure they were seen by him and his family.

"Hello, Ana. Hello, Zora," he said.

"Hello," Ana replied, a little too loud.

Aunt Celine's refrain played on a loop in Zora's head:

"Christophe is from a wonderful family."

"Your children would be beautiful."

"You would be well taken care of."

"They are New Orleans's first colored sugar-barons."

Christophe Bechet Jr. was perfect on paper. And his face was perfect in front of her: straight white teeth, perfect haircut, beautiful brown skin, and a clever smile. She could marry him. She could learn to love him...and maybe actually ease into it. He was prideful but easy to be fond of.

But he didn't make her heart race, and his wasn't the face she saw every night before she went to sleep. It was like Phillip filled a void she hadn't realized was there, like a perfect harmony sliding into place.

And now she and Christophe had to play a game where they both acted like they didn't know that an engagement was coming.

Zora tried not to cringe, remembering his kiss, which she wasn't sure he realized was unrequited. She nodded her hello.

"How have you both been?" he asked.

Ana rattled off a thousand things, and he nodded patiently as she told him way more than anyone should possibly know about your day.

"And how about you, Zora?"

"Fine." Nerves were making her feet tap. This was the *last* place she wanted to be right now.

"Zora, would you mind taking a walk with me before everything begins?" Christophe asked, reaching out a hand. Ana's eyes burned into the side of her cheek.

Zora wanted to say no. Just for Ana's sake, if nothing else. But she couldn't refuse him. Not with so many eyes on her. She took his hand, and they headed into the lobby.

"How have you been? Your aunt said you were too busy for calls last week." He leaned in close. "And you haven't been at the Petit Sapphire."

"I've been busy helping my aunt fill her orders," Zora lied, then turned away from him so he couldn't see her face. She gazed into one of the gold-rimmed mirrors that jutted from the walls and started to fuss with her hair. Her lack of sleep showed on her face. The humidity made her curls swell. Her hair puffed a little around the temples. She readjusted her cloche hat.

"I have a surprise for you."

Zora's stomach sank. "Oh, really?"

The proposal.

Every girl's dream.

Ana's dream.

She slid the ring on her right hand instead of her left, the one hidden beneath her glove so no one could see.

"What is it?" she asked, playing along. She couldn't shatter his heart. She couldn't attend this ball. They'd have to leave before it began.

"You'll have to wait and see." Chimes sounded from the main room. "Shall we return?"

Zora nodded and let him lead her back. Music poured out from a beautiful band. These last few weeks had made her crave playing more than anything. She'd been so cooped up without it. The sound of the music sent tremors under her skin, waking up her magic.

Mrs. Moore clapped her hands and gently directed everyone to take their partners.

Zora nodded. "You know my cousin will be very upset to see this."

"Upset about what?" Christophe led her onto the dance floor.

"She's sweet on you," Zora whispered as she felt everyone's eyes on her.

Sweat appeared on his temples. Other faces passed them by. One couple broke the choreographed waltz. Everybody pulled away from the center of the dance floor to give them room and to watch. Through the other bodies, Zora saw the boy's hand twirling the girl like the ballerina in her jewelry box. The girl's little hand fit perfectly inside his.

Her hair swirled around her. The wrongness of it sat like a weight in her chest, making her sluggish as Christophe tried to force her into step with him.

Zora wanted to dance like that with Phillip.

"Stop looking down," Christophe whispered. "I want us to make a good impression."

Her aunt's words hummed through her: *"Being with Christophe would be a fresh start."* Her mind spun like the other couples dancing alongside them.

Christophe tightened his grip around her waist, his fingers suddenly a vise.

"Please excuse me. I'm not feeling well." She broke away from him, dodging between people and bumping some couples off beat. She felt Christophe on her heels, but zigzagged in and out of moving people until she shot through the door.

THE LUPINE JAZZ GROUP

    January 10, 1929

    Dear Zora Broussard,

    We are thrilled that you've accepted our offer to be an artist-in-residence at the Lupine.

    You will be performing at our premier clubs four nights a week to start, beginning on Thursday, February 28, to give you time to get settled out here in the Bay Area.

    We look forward to your arrival.

    Sincerely,

    Nigel Winsome

20

*Z*ora paced around in circles in her aunt's dress room. After what happened at the rehearsal, she wasn't allowed out of the house for anything at all. Days turned to weeks. The Mardi Gras season ramped up as February neared.

Fabrics in golds and greens and purples choked the room, and a mountain of paper order forms for her aunt's signature Mardi Gras dresses sat on the desk. The phone hadn't stopped ringing since New

Year's Day. She clutched Phillip's latest letter to her chest. She couldn't stand being away from him. The date of Rocco's delivery was still a week away. She would have to go through with the krewe ball. And yet if she stayed until midnight, there would be no way for her to avoid Christophe's proposal. She wasn't sure how she'd be able to sneak away with all that attention.

The cat stared at her. "What are we going to do?" she asked. "I can't stay locked up in here much longer."

The door snapped open, and in marched her aunt. "Take the plum dress from the rack. Your future family is coming over for dinner."

"Now?"

"For your own good. To set you straight. To get rid of all that foolishness in you."

Zora crossed her hands over her chest. "I can't marry him, Auntie."

"I'm not speaking French, young lady. You will accept his offer, and we will set the wedding for the spring before the heat truly settles on top of us. You'll make a beautiful bride. Then all that music nonsense can be put away where it belongs, and you can focus on being a good wife and welcoming more of God's children."

"I c-can't," Zora stammered, her thoughts consumed with Phillip.

Aunt Celine's stinging eyes scanned her. "You look perfectly capable to me. And while you're living well on my hospitality, you'll do whatever I've asked you to do. Now fix your face and be in that sitting room with a smile." She dug her nails into Zora's shoulders and pivoted her like a spinning top.

There was no use in fighting it. Zora was swept into the bath by Mabel, dressed, and led down to the sitting room like the perfect little doll her aunt wanted her to be.

Zora lingered in the foyer, thinking about how she might escape. No one would hear her leave in Oma's shoes.

"You look beautiful tonight," came a voice from behind her.

Zora whipped around. "Thank you."

Zora welcomed Christophe with a warm, false smile and fielded the stares from his father and aunties. Her mind raced with all the ways she could still get out of this.

Aunt Celine ushered them into the sitting room while Mabel finished setting the table for dinner. Zora noticed how her aunt's worst bragging instinct came out around these women. She started to boast about the new drapes she'd put up in the house or rave about a new famous client asking her to make a dress.

Christophe Bechet Jr.'s mother circled Zora like a vulture. She was impossibly beautiful, much like Jo: skin the color of honey macarons, eyes like emeralds, and a perfectly pink mouth.

"My grandchildren will be blessed with a pleasant exterior. But what about your disposition? I need them to be advantageously skilled. This is the thing that worries me the most about you. But your aunt assures me that you are smart and talented and . . . most of all, obedient." Mrs. Bechet arched an eyebrow.

Zora dropped her gaze and bit back a retort. "Yes, ma'am." She had to play along.

"My firstborn is very important to me. I won't have anyone toying with his heart," the older woman replied.

"I would never do that," Zora lied, the bitterness of it coating her tongue.

"I know you wouldn't. Because then you'd have to deal with me." Mrs. Bechet's hazel eyes studied her, and Zora felt like she could see every curl on her head. "I don't know if you're deserving. It is yet to be seen."

One of Christophe's aunts eased back into the foyer to join them. "Adele, my chérie, is this her? Is this who will end up with our love, our Christophe?" The hat she wore twinkled with celestial shapes—the moon, the stars, the sun. Her rich brown skin glittered, and her gown trailed her like a dark wave of stardust.

"Zora Broussard, this is Christophe's aunt. My eldest sister, Maria-Christina."

Zora plastered on her best smile as she was inspected again.

The two women started to clap. "Our beloved. Our sweet."

Zora turned to find Christophe directly behind her.

"Your almost-fiancé," Mrs. Bechet said, pulling her son into the biggest hug. She left smudges of lipstick on his cheeks. "My sweet baby."

Throughout tea and dinner, they discussed the wedding as if it was a done deal. Aunt Celine put forth colors, and Mrs. Bechet began to meal-plan. His aunties added more and more people to a potential guest list. All while Zora tried not to vomit up all of Mabel's delicious food and Christophe smiled warmly at her.

After they were safely gone, Aunt Celine locked her back in the dressing room.

"I still don't trust you," she said, tucking the key into her brassiere. "There's a chamber pot in the closet. You won't be leaving here until tomorrow."

Zora paced back and forth, trying the long windows again. But they wouldn't budge. She listened for footsteps, and each time they sounded like someone other than her aunt.

She softly knocked on the door.

No answer.

She knocked again.

After the third attempt, it creaked open. Ana's face appeared. "I came to see how pitiful you looked."

Zora groaned. Not Mabel, and her cousin would definitely snitch on her if she tried to run. But maybe if she just asked her nicely, perhaps she'd soften. She took a deep breath. She didn't have a choice.

"I need a favor," Zora admitted.

"You always need something, Zora, and you don't give anything in return." Her dark eyes found Zora's in the mirror. "You even came down here and got the most eligible bachelor. You'll be the first engagement of the season. The richest colored girl in all of New Orleans."

"I just need a few hours outside of the house without your mama knowing, and I'll give you anything."

"Anything?" Ana's eyebrow lifted.

"What do you want? Name it."

Ana's mouth twitched. "I want him."

"Who?"

"Christophe. I want you to turn his proposal down. I want *him* to choose me." Ana's eyes locked with Zora's in the mirror. "No one ever chooses me. I'm always behind Evelyn or Mama...and now, *you*." Hurt flickered in her eyes, and for the first time, Zora felt like she was really seeing Ana. She was more than the annoying little cousin who was spoiled and pushy and entitled. She had a layer of feelings deep down that no one had bothered to ask about.

Christophe's warm smile flooded her mind.

"Deal."

Ana's mouth dropped open with surprise. "You'd give him up that easily?"

"He's lovely. Wonderful even. Would make for a perfect husband, but I don't love him. I never have. It would be unfair to him."

Ana smirked.

Zora didn't look back as she raced down the block in her red shoes. Ana had given her three whole hours of freedom. She held one of Phillip's letters, her thumb tracing the raised address in the top left-hand corner.

She barreled onto a streetcar, hurtling to the back, and asked a nice colored man about the address on the envelope. He told her it was in the Garden District, in the front of town where most of the uppity white folks lived, on the river. The same neighborhood Zora, Jo, and Phillip sang in at the garden party a few months ago.

Phillip had never mentioned that his family lived there. There were so many things they didn't know about each other. She wondered if there would ever be enough time to learn.

She stepped off the streetcar and onto Phillip's street. As all the white folks turned to look, fear rippled across her skin. She didn't look the part; the other colored women were in starched maid uniforms. She hadn't thought this out. How would she just show up there? Someone might say something to her. Someone might ask her to leave. Someone might call the police.

She steeled herself. "Deep breath," she whispered, turning left on his block. The houses were lined up like decadent petit-fours, blush pink, sunset orange, robin's-egg blue, seafoam green. She took tentative steps forward, looking for the house numbers.

In some New Orleans houses, children probably woke to the aroma of Saturday morning biscuits and gravy, and in some cases, a salty piece of ham. But Zora thought most mornings Phillip must've awoken to a feast of freshly powdered beignets and towers of waffles and layers of crêpes and pyramids of fresh fruit, and really, anything his heart desired.

The world darkened as Zora reached the end of the block. Her first real glimpse of the property filled her with a grave chill. The house stood tucked in the back, enveloped in a fortress of bayou trees and iron gates and locked doors. It seemed like the kind of place folks would whisper about, like its inhabitants had closed themselves off from the city, protecting the house's contents from the outside. An iron gate with black peaks seemed to whisper, "Move on—we don't want you here." Long stretches of the bayou trees arched overhead, turning the entry into the mouth of a cave.

At the gate, a wrought-iron crest spelled out *Deveraux*. A braided cord hung below.

There was the sudden sound of footsteps, and Zora jumped back. She moved around the corner, peering out to watch a Black man in a gray suit emerge from the gate. He put on his hat while fumbling with some empty boxes, then started walking in the other direction.

Zora paused, waiting until he was out of sight. Then she headed back to the foreboding entrance. Looking both ways, she tried her luck with the rope, and in the distance, she heard a chime.

A new man appeared. He had waxy white skin and dull eyes like a doll's. He inserted a large skeleton key into a wheel-shaped lock and turned it three perfect revolutions with a series of clanks. The gate opened like a mouth. Half of the iron beams disappeared into the earth, while the others lifted up toward the sky.

"What is your business here?"

"A delivery," Zora lied.

"The back," he directed, pointing. His head dropped, chin resting on his chest as if he'd fallen asleep while standing up

She hesitated for a moment before walking through the gate. Then the man swung it closed, throwing them into a darkness created by the overgrown plants and trees.

Her stomach twisted. She was trespassing. Colored people were arrested, hurt, and killed for things like this. She would stick to her delivery story if she saw any other person and hope that Phillip was here. The thought of Phillip's face was the only prize at the end of this dangerous mission.

Ahead, the expanse of the house emerged like a sleeping monster hidden from view. Enormous glass windows released an anemic yellow glow as their lids rose like eyes. The porch was a row of broken teeth, its wood chipped and fragmented. As she walked the path to the back door, long-stemmed flowers hung upside down, their petals cracked and dried.

She made her way around back. The door creaked open. She swallowed all the fear, the little voice that said she shouldn't be entering a white person's home without permission.

She was unprepared for the dishes stacked in dangerous towers, soot-streaked fireplaces hoarding last winter's ashes, tipsy sofas and their drunken wobbles, and how every imaginable surface, every wall and furniture top, was piled with everything and anything from garlic to lanterns to buckets to bolts of lace to empty violin cases to half-burned candles to eyeglass lenses to the severed limbs of dolls.

Black drapes covered each wall and window. Wooden floors creaked beneath her feet.

"Hello?" she whispered.

No answer.

Voices escaped from a nearby room, and against her better judgment, she followed them.

There sat an ancient-looking family of three around a dining room table. They ate in silence, chewing their food and staring into their plates. An old woman in a heaping pile of black fabric had chalky skin that was so translucent Zora could see her network of veins. Beside her sat a large white man with a mustache that hung over his lip like its very own awning. Thick sadness stretched across that massive mahogany table. She could remember the roar of laughter and the warmth of Mama's oven and how Mama had to remind her daddy to eat before the food got cold because he talked so much at the table.

Zora looked for Phillip, realizing he was the young man whose back was turned. When he tilted his head, she found him, sullen and sad. Unrecognizable. His jovial manner muted. Her heart did a somersault. She wanted to reach out and touch him, to make him laugh and see that easy smile she was so used to.

Suddenly, a server dropped platters of food before the family and walked in her direction. Zora froze.

Sweat soaked her brow, and she gazed around for a place to hide. Too late. Zora stood there; a mouse caught in a trap. She thought about the servant who had let her in, who would certainly be suspicious about her delivery story if she were found inside the house. The magic inside her flared—a warm, tingly feeling spread through her limbs. The woman rushed past her as if she were nothing more than a ghost.

"Didn't see you there, Jeffrey," she called over her shoulder. "Did you put the deliveries in the kitchen? Your tip is on the table."

Zora gazed down. Her body seemed different for a split second—a flash of longer legs, loafers, and gray pants instead of her blue skirt. And then, just like that, she was back to her normal self.

Could it be... Was this part of her magic? Could she not only move things at will, but also hide—or perhaps disguise herself? There was so much she didn't know. There was so much her mama and Oma never told her.

Phillip excused himself, leaving almost a plateful of food behind. He slipped from the dining room and strode down the hall.

She breathed in his scent, her heart swelling as she tugged at the back of his shirt.

He whipped back around. "Who's there?"

"Me," she whispered.

Phillip scrambled backward. "How?"

"Hi."

Looking around quickly, he pulled her into a side room and closed the door behind them.

"Zora," he breathed as she glanced around the dark room filled with stuffy furniture. A used tea set sat on an old wooden table.

They looked at each other. Zora suddenly felt shy, the months apart swimming between them, the anticipation of trying to fit a lifetime into a couple of hours.

He pulled her into a kiss, and sparks tingled across her limbs. "How did you get out of your aunt's house?"

"My cousin Ana covered for me. Only for a little while." She kissed him again, unable to help herself. She refocused. "I came to tell you— you have to pick me up earlier than midnight on the fifth. Eight o'clock, maybe nine at the latest. Before the dance is in full swing."

"Why?"

"Christophe is going to propose to me that night. I don't want to have to turn him down in front of everyone. I need to speak to him privately beforehand."

"You're an engaged woman."

"*I* know that, but the world doesn't. My aunt is still hell-bent on it. She's practically got my firstborn kid named already. Anyway, I think the plan will still work. We'll be able to sneak away while everyone is distracted by the party, just a bit earlier. Before all eyes are on us." She paused, excited to tell him the rest. "And Mr. Winsome finally wrote back! I start my residency end of February."

Phillip whistled low. "That's wonderful, Zora. It's all coming together." He nibbled his bottom lip the way he always did when he was thinking. "Let me talk to Rocco, see if the priest can come earlier; we'll make it work. Maybe he can get us train tickets for that night, too." He squeezed her hands. "I can't wait to marry you, to start our lives together. A hurricane couldn't stop me."

"Do you think Rocco can manage it?"

"Yes. . . ." A cloud passed over his face.

"What?"

"He wants me to become his partner. Thinks my family connections might help. He's trying to find a way to get the Fratellos to take him seriously and give him more responsibilities. He thinks I'll make him look good to the bosses."

"Bootlegging?" She didn't like the idea of Phillip doing illegal things or being like Rocco. All of those things ended up bad.

"Don't worry."

"I have to worry. Isn't that what wives do?"

He leaned forward, beckoning her for a kiss. She submitted, kissing him again, then slipped out of his arms.

Phillip shrugged. "I found a way to help him without doing all of that. I promised him my car as a thank-you."

She inhaled. "But you love that car."

"I love you more. And my promise to you is most important." The feeling of his breath on her neck sent tremors through her.

"Phillip?" a muffled voice called from outside the door.

Zora tensed.

"Everything is fine, Mother," Phillip called loudly.

There was a bit of shuffling, and then all was quiet.

Phillip looked at the tea set. "They'll probably be in to clean in a bit. We should go."

Her heart thudding in her ears, Zora took his hand as they moved toward the door.

A hallway stretched before them, winding narrowly like a dark river. They passed by a gigantic family portrait on the wall: a young woman holding a baby boy in her lap, a mustached man beside her. Next to it, there was the family crest Phillip had mentioned—a tangle of colors and the star-shaped flowers. They walked through a music room with a half-rotted piano whose ribs and innards showed. The skeletons of violins and guitars were scattered about the walls; only their frames and strings remained, the rest eaten by time. Music wafted down a double staircase.

He opened a door.

What had to be his room spread out before her. Sheet music sat in towers among a sea of different instruments. A baby grand piano sat closest to the French doors leading out to a terrace.

His hands slid on top of hers, and he pressed her fingers down on the keys. They played a tune they'd just started writing for their next set at the Petit Sapphire. The music swirled around them.

Phillip kissed along Zora's neck, and his fingers found the line of buttons on her dress. He undid each and left a kiss after. A trail of warmth made the hair on her arms stand up.

"I wish we could leave for San Francisco right now," she whispered.

"I do, too, but I want to travel with you when you're my wife." He took her hand in his and admired the beautiful ring he'd put on it weeks ago. He removed it from the right ring finger and placed it on the left. "It'll live on this finger soon."

They started to kiss, soft and slow, then deeper, more urgent. It was like they were making up for lost time and trying to block everything that stood in their way with the pureness and ferocity of their love.

He took her hand and led her to his bed. She fumbled with the buttons on his shirt. Finally, they lay side by side. Her eyes combed over his skin, alabaster freckled with caramel drops, and hers so different, rich chestnut brown. The contrast made the lines white folks had drawn between colored and white even more visible. Her heart drummed through her entire body. "I missed you," she whispered as he pressed on top of her.

"I missed you, too." He kissed his promise into her skin.

Zora and Phillip slept, legs tangled together, hearts still pattering with the rhythm of their love, and dreams full of what was next for them.

21

he night of the debutante ball swept in like a storm, sudden and bigger than expected. Aunt Celine's house swarmed with girls with last-minute emergencies, needing a hem fixed or a hole patched or another train of beads. Zora ran her fingers over the beaded neckline of her blush-pink gown. She'd gotten a letter from Phillip that Rocco had bought tickets for the overnight sleeper train. She would leave the ball just before eight p.m.—right as the festivities really began. They'd swing by her aunt's to pick up her things. Then she'd be married to Phillip in this gown, wearing Oma's shoes, before heading to the station.

Her cat nosed around her legs and ducked its head beneath her bed, where her valise sat packed and ready. "Don't give me away." She picked the cat up and put him on the bed.

"Who *is* going to give you away, Zora?" Evelyn asked. "Mama says you're getting engaged tonight. Will your daddy come down from New York?" She twirled around in her light green gown.

The memory of Papa's eyes felt faint.

"Of course he would," Ana added, playing along.

Zora's promise to Ana stretched between them. She would turn Christophe Bechet Jr. down early and suggest he marry Ana. She would leave forever. She would be with the love of her life; the only person she'd ever loved outside of her parents and Oma. It would be a fresh start—for both of them. Away from the magic and the visions and the hatred, and toward the music.

"I wonder how he'll ask," Evelyn said. "I've always wanted a romantic proposal."

Zora thought of Phillip's proposal. How it was both simple and romantic. The question whispered in her ear, tickling across her skin and settling into her bones like it was always supposed to be true. She didn't need a big loud love; a quiet and steady one would do.

"I want to get a new hair ribbon." Ana left the room.

"Do you want to get married?" Zora asked Evelyn after her sister was gone.

Evelyn jumped, the question a hot poker. "Yes," she whispered.

Zora waited for her to fill in the rest of it.

"But I don't know if I will be able to."

"Why?"

"It isn't allowed."

In this moment, Zora wished she could tell her about Phillip. How her love for him wasn't "allowed" either, but it was still there no matter how hard she tried to fight it.

"Anaïs is too afraid."

The realization washed over Zora, and she reached out to squeeze Evelyn's hand. Evelyn looked in the opposite direction, fighting back tears.

The bedroom door snapped open.

Evelyn dropped Zora's hand.

Aunt Celine and Ana marched in. "Girls, girls, why aren't you dressed? It's almost time to go."

Zora pulled the gown over her silk slip. Aunt Celine buttoned her. "Zora."

She braced for her aunt's bite, turning around slowly, but found her staring back with soft eyes. "Tonight's a big one for you." She pulled a string of pearls from her pocket and brushed a warm hand across Zora's collarbone. "This will be something borrowed for you. You deserve to look your most beautiful on such a night. One that will change your life."

Guilt suddenly flooded Zora's stomach. Her aunt had done so much for her. Taken her in. Fed her. Gave her some slivers of momentary kindness. Now she'd disobey her in the largest of ways. "Thank you," she whispered as her aunt draped the pearls across her neck. She told herself that she'd make it up to her somehow.

"Very pretty. Just what you needed. Don't be nervous." She patted her shoulder and pivoted Zora around for Evelyn and Ana to see. "Doesn't she look nice, girls?"

If Ana's eyes could burn, they'd have left a scorch along Zora's neckline. Zora wished she could take the pearls off and hand it all to Ana right now, including Christophe Bechet Jr.'s proposal.

The Magnolia Hotel sparkled. A parade float sat right outside, ready to carry the debs through the streets to celebrate the girl who would be crowned, and horses whinnied and neighed as their manes were decorated. Candles twinkled in every corner, and garlands in purple, gold, and green hung from every balcony. Velvet settees waited for groups of people to sit and chat, while carved banquet tables of teak and orange blossom wood held magnolias, roses, and jasmine flowers, leaving their ubiquitous and heady scents. Tuxedoed servers whizzed about the room with fragrant food. Under the chandeliers, debutantes shimmered like macarons lined up in the patisserie's shelves: delicate, rich, and expensive.

Aunt Celine kissed the cheeks of well-dressed men and women as they made their way inside. Ana and Evelyn gazed all around, oohing and ahhing at every turn. A band played soft music as everyone milled about, talking and laughing and admiring each other's gowns.

A nervous tremor continued in Zora's belly. Her head was buzzing with Phillip's plan—*sneak out before the dance starts, and he and Rocco would be waiting in the car to take them to get married*—and her guilt about embarrassing Christophe and letting her aunt down. But Ana's eyes continued to find her, reminding her of the promise.

Zora located the dessert tables and helped herself to a series of pastries, hoping the sugar would provide the spike of courage she needed.

Christophe found her stuffing herself.

Panic coursed through her veins alongside the magic. It was time.

"How are you?" he asked.

"Fine," she said, trying not to let her voice come off too clipped, too strange. She had to remain calm and act as if everything was all right. She just had to make it through the first part of the evening.

"You look pretty," he offered.

"So do you. I mean, you look handsome," she said.

He laughed, then she laughed, too. He *was* handsome, and he was all right. He'd make a wonderful husband for Ana or any other young woman who ended up with him. "Can we talk in private?" He'd beat her to it.

Zora braced herself as she followed Christophe out of the room. Ana's gaze found hers, and Zora nodded. Christophe led her into a billiards room and closed the door.

She gulped. "I know what it is...and...and—"

She didn't want to hurt him. He deserved a great love story with someone who loved him deeply.

He took a ring box from an inner pocket in his jacket. But before he could open it and ask the question, Zora put her hand on the box. "Please...I can't."

Confusion marred his face. "I haven't even asked you yet."

"But before you do, just don't, all right?" Zora tried to soften her voice.

"Don't ask you to marry me?"

"Right."

His expression darkened. "Why?"

The image of Phillip appeared in her mind. "You don't want to marry me. You don't love me."

"Love takes time," he said.

"I'm not who you think I am. I'm not the right fit. I won't make you happy."

"How do you know that?" His grip on the box tightened.

"I know myself. I know who I am." She tried to touch his hand.

He took a step back, and his mouth pursed. His pride had been stung. "Is there someone else?"

She gazed at the floor.

"Who?"

"You don't know him," she replied.

"I know a lot of people," he challenged, his voice hurt. "And I know who you are, too, Sweet Willow." A threat lingered beneath his words. "This isn't about me . . . is it? Admit it. Tell the truth."

Zora froze, and she went cold, the hairs on her skin rising.

"Is it someone at the Petit Sapphire?" he asked.

When she didn't reply, he continued. "The owner? Or one of the musicians? Surely not . . ."

She looked up for half a second, but it gave her away.

"It's about that white man on the piano." His voice rose with anger. "Yes, okay, I see now. I remember the way you looked at him when you played together."

"Yes," she admitted.

"And you love him? A white man?" he spat. "Even after all the things *they* do to colored people? Even though it's against the law—a law *they* created?"

His words hit her one after the other, like pelted bricks. She couldn't argue with him. He wasn't wrong. Her love for Phillip was improbable. It was a gamble. It wasn't what she'd planned for. It was probably the worst thing for her to explore.

But she loved Phillip. The music he played on the piano drifted through her, as fresh and strong as the memory of his scent. He was part of her now, no way to root it out.

"I love him," she said. The words were still hard to say aloud.

His eyes narrowed to slits. "You think the world will accept you? You think he can give you the things I can give you?"

"Christophe, I'm sorry."

"What am I supposed to tell everyone? My mother? Your aunt? My aunts? The whole crowd? Our community? Everyone knew we were to be married." He shook his head and burst out of the room.

A dreadful weight sat in her stomach.

The grandfather clock in the room struck eight p.m. Zora waited for Phillip, looking out the window for the shiny red car. He was late.

Phillip and Rocco were supposed to be waiting for her at the back of the hotel. There was still time to grab her valise and cat from her aunt's house and go marry Phillip before the train left at ten. But where was he?

She couldn't keep going between the bathroom and back room, hiding from Aunt Celine while she waited. Still, as the debutantes were called to the dance floor at the center of the room, she inched left, squeezing between the eager bodies, whispering *Excuse me*, and telling a few who flashed her perplexed looks that her stomach hurt.

"One of our lovely gentlemen has a word to share with us before we continue with our festivities," Mrs. Annabelle Fournier announced.

"Good evening," Christophe's voice boomed.

The girls around her clapped and jumped with excitement. Some whispered about how handsome he was, others theorized that maybe he was announcing his engagement, and still others swooned.

Zora, on her way to the bathroom to hide again, froze still as a statue. She whipped around to face the stage.

"With the coming of Lent and a period of reflection, I've been trying to live in the light. The whole city is celebrating and engaging in its yearly debauchery. Yet we should think about what this period is actually about. The continued celebration of our Lord." He made the sign of the cross.

Zora and Christophe didn't break eye contact. A smug smile danced over his lips.

"My gracious and beautiful mother gave me my grand-mère's ring to propose to a girl tonight."

There was a series of gasps of excitement. What was he doing? Was he going to ask her *now*? The magic inside Zora flared alongside her rage. Her eyes narrowed as she stared at Christophe. All she could see was his smug grin.

"But I discovered she was a fraud. Zora Broussard, the niece of Celine Broussard, is living a double life as a tawdry singer named Sweet Willow at the Petit Sapphire. She brings disgrace and sin to the Original Carolina Club. It's no telling what else she's doing at those clubs. They aren't places for distinguished young ladies."

The girls around her gasped. The men turned to gawk. As Aunt Celine strode in her direction, the adults were nodding and harrumphing in agreement.

Zora couldn't believe he was doing this to her. She'd thought he was a good man. Thought he cared about her, at least a little. But all he cared about was his pride. And now there would be no sneaking away.

Her dream of a life with Phillip was over. Just like that.

The rage inside her exploded. All directed at Christophe. Her magic burst from her hands in one hot wave. She lifted him from the stage and dangled him above the crowd as if he were no more than a brown hot-air balloon.

Everyone screamed and ducked. Some dropped to their knees in prayer. Others shouted of the devil.

Banquet tables flipped over. Glass shattered. People tumbled left and right, their terrified screams ripping through the room. Chandeliers crashed from the domed ceiling like fallen stars.

She knocked over one of the room's columns as her aunt screamed.

Zora felt hands around her waist, snapping her out of her focused fervor. She dropped Christophe on the velvet settees with a thud.

It was her cousin Evelyn.

Zora's knees started to buckle. She let her cousin drag her limp body from the room. The hallway was chaos, people running in a thousand directions. Glass shards had ripped slices into her gown, and she was soaked in sweat.

"I don't know what that was, but you have to go now!" Evelyn shouted. "Get out of here."

Her words startled Zora out of her trance. She nodded, knowing she would never see Evelyn again.

"Thank you." Zora wasn't sure if she even said the words aloud, but she hoped Evelyn knew.

22

Screams followed Zora as she threw open the back door, silently praying Phillip would finally be there. As promised, he sat in his red car, with Jo and Rocco, but his smile quickly turned to a frown of concern.

"Get her in the car," Rocco yelled from the driver's seat, looking at the chaos in front of him. "Quick, quick."

They piled Zora into the backseat. Jo sat up front with Rocco, and Phillip cradled Zora's head in his lap.

"What happened?" Jo shouted as they peeled away.

Exhaustion and adrenaline made her words thick as cane syrup as she slowly told the story. Then her eyelids fluttered, and she passed out in Phillip's arms.

Hours later, Zora was startled awake. The scene around her sharpened: several beds squeezed into a small room, trunks spilling their contents, a vanity overrun with all manner of beauty products, and a single lamp on the nightstand. She sat up and put her feet on the rough floor.

The door squeaked open. Phillip's pale white face poked in. "You're awake." He rushed to her side, his eyes combing over her. "How do you feel?"

"Where are we?"

"This is Jo's house. Her mother and sisters are at another ball."

Zora gazed all around. She'd never been to Jo's house in Storyville before. The house felt so different from her aunt's: chipped paint and worn floorboards. "What happened?" she asked weakly.

"We don't know. We were waiting for you in the alley behind the Magnolia Hotel, and you came barreling out. Your dress was ripped, and you were hysterical."

Zora closed her eyes and braced herself as memories of the night came rushing back: the debutantes, the gowns, the proposal, Christophe Bechet Jr.'s announcement, her rage.

"Christophe decided to tell the entire room that I am Sweet Willow and that I am disgusting and have no morals and am unfit to be a debutante. I lost control." Tears streamed down her cheeks. "Again."

A wave of grief welled over her. Her magic was still smoldering inside of her, still dangerous as ever. "Are you sure you want to marry someone who can do what I do? Who can't keep their temper? Who may get you in trouble?"

A smile lit up his face. "It'll keep things interesting when we're exhausted from running after babies."

Zora blinked. She hadn't given much thought to children. She hadn't given much thought to many things, it seemed. But the thought of a family with Phillip erased some of the abject terror she felt about what happened tonight.

She stared at him, incredulous.

"So, will you still marry me?" he asked.

She looked down at her tattered gown. "Like this? Here? Now? Is there time?"

"Yes. Just like that."

"But I look terrible."

The door opened again. "That's why I'm here." Jo burst in, holding a lacy cream dress. "I'll get you ready in no time."

"I paid the priest to wait. He's downstairs. Everything is ready. We still have a little over an hour. We'll get married, swing by your aunt's, and head to the station." Phillip leaned forward and waited for her to meet him halfway for a kiss. She brushed her lips against his. "Nothing is stopping me from heading into the moonlight with you." He hummed a bit of "Moonlight," their song.

"Now, Phillip, out with you. I need to make Zora a beautiful bride." Jo rushed him out of the room and locked the door with a click.

Zora and Phillip stood in the tiny plot of land behind Jo's house. Every candle had been taken outside to make a pathway to a set of crates. There stood an old priest; the wrinkles on his face reminded Zora of a molasses cookie.

Jo and Rocco stood at their side.

Zora held Phillip's hand and gazed into his blue eyes.

Zora had never been to a wedding before, so she wasn't sure how this one measured up. It was quick yet beautiful. Her heart felt full, and everything felt right.

The priest said the vows for them to repeat to each other. Phillip couldn't stop smiling the entire time, and Zora felt like she was on the edge of a chuckle. She loved the way his eyes smiled just like his mouth, tiny creases in the corners, reminding her that he was truly and deeply happy.

"You may now kiss your bride," the priest said.

Phillip kissed her hand first like he always did, then pulled her close and kissed her soft at first and then deeper. All the noises of New Orleans drifted away. The sound of cicadas. The sound of car honks. The sound of folks yelling on the street about this thing and that.

It was just the two of them, the candlelight flickering across their skin, and the smell of all the magnolias and sweet roses Jo had put in her hair.

Rocco clapped and whistled.

Phillip smiled again, disrupting the most perfect kiss Zora had ever received.

Jo rushed to her and kissed both her cheeks. "Congratulations. I'm so happy for you."

As soon as it was done, they piled into the red car and left for Aunt Celine's house to grab Zora's suitcase and her cat. Rocco drove them through the back-a-town. He turned the lights off as they got closer to the house.

The streets swelled with people headed to and from parties. The sound of police sirens echoed.

"Wait," Zora said, leaning forward. "Look. They're all at my aunt's house."

"We can't stop," Phillip said.

"Get down," Jo said. "Quick."

Zora crouched on the floorboard and held her breath as the car eased past.

Her heart sank. She'd have to leave her precious cat behind. Phillip reached out and gripped her hand.

"I'll get you another one," he whispered.

But she knew there would be no other cat like that one.

Her last connection to Oma.

"Go straight to the station, Rocco," Phillip said.

Rocco drove them to Union Station. Late-night passengers ready to board sleeper trains shuffled through the archway.

Phillip took his valise from the trunk and set it on the sidewalk.

Zora hugged Jo and rocked back and forth, making her giggle and laugh.

"I'm going to miss you," Jo said as tears coated her light eyes.

"I am, too. There's nobody like you." She touched her cheek. "You didn't know me from Adam when I first got here, and that didn't matter to you."

"I won't be able to sing with anyone else," Jo said.

"You will." Zora kissed her cheek. "You have a beautiful voice. My lark."

A pink blush deepened the one Jo wore. "You flatter me."

"Because it's true."

Phillip handed Rocco the keys to the car. Rocco flashed his greasy grin. Zora hugged him. Despite her fears, her suspicions about him had proved unfounded. She felt bad for thinking such awful thoughts of him. He'd come through for them when it mattered.

They waved goodbye, and Phillip and Zora walked into the train station, ready to start their new life.

Zora took a deep breath and took her ticket from Phillip. On it was a stamp: *colored*. "I'll see you there."

They started to head toward the platform.

"I'll be waiting for—" Phillip froze. "Don't move."

Zora flinched. "What is it?"

He stepped closer to her, talking under his breath. "The place is full of policemen. They're holding Wanted posters. Don't turn around."

"What's going on?" A tremor shot through her.

"Your face is on one—and so is mine."

Zora pulled her cloche hat down and took out her fan. She looked left at one of the policemen plastering the Wanted poster of her and Phillip's faces to the wall. She squinted her eyes to read the charges: *Last seen fleeing the Magnolia Hotel after starting a fire*.

"We have to walk out slowly. We can't act alarmed," Phillip said.

"All right." She took a deep breath. "We can go back to Jo's, then figure out what to do. We can't leave tonight."

He squeezed her hand. "Let's separate. I'll meet you across the street."

She nodded.

They walked out, moving slowly, and headed in different directions—past policemen interviewing passengers ready to board the last train to leave for the night.

The train they should have been on.

23

Zora paced back and forth in Jo's small living room. Her mind
was a tangle of worries about what happened after she left
the Magnolia Hotel. What had she done?

Outside, she could hear Phillip talking to Rocco. "We have to get
rid of the car," Phillip said.

"But it's mine now," Rocco protested. "I need it."

"The police are looking for it. They'll find it . . . and you . . . and then
us." Phillip raised his hands, exasperated.

"Stop arguing," Jo interrupted. "We have to get you out of here before my maman comes home. She'll call the police on us all."

"Where are we going to go?" Zora said, panicked. They couldn't get a hotel room together. None would allow colored guests.

"You have to leave the city a different way," Jo said. She sat up. "Hey, there's always that Europe idea."

"How?" Zora asked.

Rocco nodded slowly. "A ship leaves every month. One should go out next week."

"How do you know?" Zora asked.

"Trust me, I know every ship in and out of this city, sweetheart." His greasy smile was back.

"Remember I showed you the schedule?" Jo continued. "It's the one I wanted to go on. Your marriage would be legal. One of my aunts lives there with her white husband." Jo rushed to the window. "We should leave. They'll be coming home any minute now."

"The Fratellos have a place I can take you. It's at the edge of Orleans Parish. Boss likes it that way. But he'll be back in town before too long. And I'll need that car . . . or something better. I already told him about it."

"We'll figure something out." Phillip pressed his hands together like he was saying a prayer. "Thank you, thank you. I owe you again."

Rocco nodded stiffly.

They piled into Phillip's car, and Rocco drove them out of the French Quarter and to the very edge of the city. Zora's heart didn't stop racing until they were far away.

The modest house sat at the back of the road, almost desolate, unremarkable. A building one wouldn't look at twice. Zora and Jo brought Phillip's suitcase inside and nosed around. The first thing Zora noticed was the sound in the small and beautiful home. Or rather the absence of it. It was as if New Orleans had disappeared and they were in a different place entirely. The moment her feet sank into the plush carpet, the noise from outside dropped to a hush. As if it were being muffled, like a heavy blanket had been drawn over the entire space, warding away the possibility of visitors, nosy neighbors ... and most importantly, any policemen.

It was a fitting house for a mob boss.

The floors and paneled walls were stained a dark mahogany. Silk drapes of a costly chartreuse hue trimmed with golden tassels framed every arched window. A chaise longue sat empty in the chamber's center, like a throne. Dust drifted, the dim light catching every fleck.

Through the window, Zora kept her eye on Phillip and Rocco as they started to argue. They walked away from the house. Phillip shoved cash in Rocco's pocket, and Rocco pushed him away. "You think they'll stop?" she asked Jo.

"No, Rocco really wants the car."

"But it's just a car."

"Maybe to you."

Her answer surprised Zora.

"Promises are promises. He was counting on it." Jo joined her at the window, watching from a distance as Rocco stomped around while Phillip lit a match and set the beautiful car on fire.

Rocco and Jo were gone by the time Phillip and Zora woke in the hideout house the next morning. Only a note remained:

P,

> *Gone to buy your passage on the next ship out of New Orleans to Paris. Leaves on Mardi Gras at midnight. Meet me there. Lay low until then.*
>
> *R*

"He's still angry with me," Phillip admitted.

"You had to get rid of the car," Zora placed a hand on his shoulder. "There was nothing we could do."

"He loved that car so much," he said with a sigh.

"Why?"

"When you don't grow up with things like that, it makes you want them. Makes you think it'll fill something inside. He's always been that way. People have overlooked him or thought he was nothing. Down here . . . having a little bit of something means no one can dismiss you."

Zora understood a lot about being overlooked and dismissed. As soon as she walked outside of her house, white people saw her and treated her as if she were a second-class citizen because of the deep brown of her skin.

"He'll forgive me. I'll give him more money to get another one."

"From where?"

"I got some from my father," he said. "From his safe."

"You took it?"

"It was mine for when I turned twenty-one. I just took it early is all." He went to his suitcase and started to unpack. He set the mirror on the bed. Zora patted the space next to her. They sat side by side. She clutched his free hand. "How does it usually work?" she asked.

"Sometimes it just shows me things. Other times I think of a question and a vision appears."

She traced her fingers along its edges. "Let me try asking something."

He handed the mirror to her.

"Are we going to be all right in Paris?" She stared at her reflection, trying to will the glass into showing her what would happen to them.

Nothing.

"Could you please show me what our lives will be like in Paris?" she asked awkwardly, but the mirror still only showed her face.

Maybe she was trying too hard.

"Let's do it together." Phillip leaned over. "Please show us what is to come." Zora inhaled and repeated the phrase, then they held the mirror together and said it in unison.

The glass grew warm in their hands as the willow tree symbol shone bright. A set of clouds skated across the surface as if they'd been plucked straight from the sky outside their window.

But then it disappeared.

The shrouded coffin appeared once more, Zora's shiny red shoes peeking through. The image filled her with more dread than it ever had before. She thought of the fortune-teller from the circus all those nights ago: *"You must relinquish it before you pay with blood."* She hadn't relinquished one bit of her magic. Would this be the price?

Seemingly equally rattled, Phillip threw the mirror on the bed and started to pace. Zora walked up behind him, slipping her arms around his waist and forcing him to settle into her.

"It's going to be all right," she whispered, willing it with her words.

"What happens if I can't protect you?" he asked. "I need to know that we're going to be all right, that *you* are." He broke from her grasp and turned to face her. "We should see my mother. She knows how the mirror works, and technically, it is hers."

"You took it from her?" Zora asked.

"She never looks at it anymore. . . . I thought it would help us."

Zora pursed her mouth in disapproval.

"At some point, I'll have to slip home to get my passport and another car from my father's storage unit for Rocco. We will need it to leave. But maybe we should see her, too—ask her what the visions mean, what we need to do to make sure they don't follow us all the way to Europe. I've had enough haunting and curses for one lifetime."

Zora's heart sank, her mind latching onto a piece of the plan that was already falling apart. "In all the hoopla, it slipped my mind that we would need papers. I don't have a passport."

Phillip lifted her chin and gazed into her eyes. "You're my wife. Wives can travel on their husband's passports as long as we have a marriage certificate."

"Our marriage is illegal—or did you forget?"

He kissed her lips.

"It isn't illegal in France, and Rocco got the certificate signed for us. A clerk owed him a favor, Mrs. Phillip Deveraux."

She pulled his mouth to hers again and bit his bottom lip. "It's Zora Deveraux. Or really, Sadie Walker Deveraux to you and only you."

He grinned. "We'll lay low here as long as we can. Then we'll stop at the house on the way to the docks." He took her hand and pulled her forward.

"Wait." She stopped. "Did you tell your parents about me?"

"Of course I did. I told them I'd met and married the love of my life, Zora Broussard. That we were leaving to start our lives together."

"But do they *know*?" she pressed.

His eyes filled with a soft sadness. "I didn't think to mention it. They were already upset that I'd eloped."

She wrenched her hand from his. "Phillip. How could you leave something like that out?"

"I don't *see* your color."

She bristled. "But it doesn't change that I have one. I don't want you to *not* see it. I'm proud of it. I can love it and you."

"But—"

Zora brushed away his words. "You touch my skin every day. You see my skin every day. Pretending it doesn't exist is a fairy tale." She shook with anger, pushing back tears and frustration. "How could you *not* tell them?"

He rushed to her, pulling her into his arms. "I'm sorry," he whispered into her hair a thousand times until her limbs went soft and she allowed him to hold her. "I'll never do that again."

"Will they hate me?" she asked in the tiniest voice.

"Probably."

She pinched him.

"But no matter what they say or how they react, you are who I want. I love you; you're my family now, and I'm yours."

The mirror glowed.

Both Phillip and Zora gazed down.

"What..." Phillip started.

Within the glass, Zora saw a new vision: a woman—one with golden hair and a lucky smile. The woman walked hand in hand with a younger version of her grandmother. Snippets of a conversation escaped: the words *Elva* and *curse* and *the power of broken promises* echoed.

"Something bad is going to happen..." she heard the girl say.

Who is that? Zora thought.

The images changed. She saw her grandmother on a ship headed for the port of New York. She heard laughter and felt her love for the brown man she'd met in a pharmacy. Her abolitionist grandfather. She watched Oma put a shroud over their brownstone. There were small glimpses of her mother as a child and then her. Stories she'd been told came to life before her eyes. Stories about a dear friend named Elva, stories that had died with her oma. Stories of magic and love her mama had buried after that loss.

"What is happening, Phillip?" she asked.

"I don't know. I've never seen these images before."

The glass darkened. The pictures fluttered. Zora pregnant, two small twin babies running through a house, a storm, a girl behind glass with red shoes.

The mirror went blank again, and Zora put a hand to her stomach, wondering.

Phillip held the mirror up as if that might conjure another image.

A cold settled in her. "What is going to happen to us?"

The sun never returned to the sky; a storm had ushered in the dusk. Zora and Phillip stared at the mirror for hours as a great black quilt spread outside the window. The mirror was blank. They both remained silent, an unease settling between the two of them about their future. Elva's words echoed inside her . . . something bad was about to happen.

24

They lay low for a few days. When Zora closed her eyes and curled up next to Phillip to sleep, she was pulled into nightmares. They were of her with two small babies lodged in the eye of tumultuous storms—hail bullets pounding their shoulders, ribbons of rain soaking their clothes, streams of running water becoming muddy lanes beneath her feet.

The hiding made her anxious. "Phillip?" She turned to his side of the bed and found a note.

My love,

   Went to get more milk and food. Safer for me than for you. Be back soon.

   Rest.

   P

Zora climbed out of bed and went to the washbasin. She wiped the sticky sweat off her limbs and glared at herself in the wall mirror. The wet nightgown clung to her, and she pulled it tight to her stomach, wondering again if those babies were already in there. Nerves skittered across her skin, and she got dressed quickly, swaddling herself in a scarf, took Phillip's mirror, and left the house before she changed her mind. Wearing her red slippers, Zora knew no one would follow her.

"I need to know that we're all going to be all right. That we're all going to be able to leave," she whispered to herself, the refrain settling down into her and momentarily quieting the worries piling up. Exhausted, brain tired and legs sore, she went straight to South Rampart Street and the AceJack Pharmacy on the corner.

The "Open" sign dangled in the window. She walked inside. "Mama B?"

The place was just as it had been the last time she'd entered: a cornucopia of the odd. The walls still held cupboards lined with bottles of every shape and size, some containing dried powders and others dried roots, liquids the color of indigo, crimson, and licorice; bulb-shaped vials; and vases of curious construction. Tables featured flasks of pickled items, iron skeleton keys bundled with silk ribbons, delicate fans, and piles of candlesticks in every color. A wingback chair held a chubby animal that wasn't quite a cat, though Zora couldn't place it and didn't remember the creature from the last time she was here. Oil lamps cast their yellow glow through the space like eyes watching for movement.

She wanted to inspect each item on each table and each cupboard shelf and read each cursive label. She wanted to remove each stopper and smell each liquid. She wanted to learn what it all was and if it could help her.

She repeated the woman's name as she inched closer and closer to the shelves, not sure she'd be able to curb her curiosity.

Mama B clucked her tongue. "And just what do you think you're doing? I'll have you know I don't tolerate snooping."

"I came to see you."

Mama B jammed a hand to her hip. "I don't do business with those who can't keep their word."

Zora took the mirror from her satchel. "I need to show you something—my husband's mirror."

"Husband?" Mama B's eyebrows lifted with surprise.

Zora blushed and stepped forward to let her hold it. "You're the only one I know that might have the answers."

Mama B took the mirror and set it on the counter. "Such beauty. Such craftsmanship. Very old and powerful." She leaned down to have a closer look, grabbing a pair of spectacles from a drawer.

Mama B released a series of surprised oohs. "The glass shows truth."

"So everything that we've seen is true?"

The mirror glowed. The shrouded woman in the coffin with the red shoes appeared.

Mama B gasped.

"Who is that?" Zora asked. "Is it me? Is an early death my fate?"

"No use in getting all worked up. That won't get the answers. Magic never responds well to force. You've learned that the hard way." Zora flinched at the thought of the Wanted posters.

"Don't worry, I have no plans on calling the law. Always in everybody's business when they should be tending to their own." Mama B traced her finger along the edge of the mirror. "I don't know who this woman is, but carrying all these charged objects"—she pointed at the red shoes on Zora's feet—"leaves a trail behind. You should let me buy them from you. I'd give you a fair price, and it would be enough money to carry you out of this place."

Zora considered the proposition. She always kept her family's magic close, kept it like a special, private jewel in the recess of her heart. She remembered her mama's words after Oma had passed—that they would be hunted and used as instruments and tools of violence and greed, regarded as creatures if the rest of the world ever discovered their magic, and that without Oma's presence there was no need to even use it.

But maybe if she and Phillip rid themselves of these objects, it would be the closest thing to getting rid of the magic itself.

"Your fear is going to catch you one day," Mama B said. "I can feel it."

She exhaled. *No.* She couldn't give up Phillip's family heirloom, especially not without speaking to him about it first. "I've made so many mistakes," Zora admitted.

"Keep them. You're not ready."

Zora put the mirror back into her bag. "I'm sorry, Mama B. I wasted your time again."

"Nothing to be sorry about. Life is too short for all the sorrys."

Zora turned to leave.

"Chérie," Mama B called out.

Zora turned back around.

"Beware of the crow and the snake." Zora froze, thinking of the fortune-teller and of the circus with that curious symbol. "There are folks nosing around the city asking questions about magic . . . and you."

25

*Z*ora rushed through the French Quarter and boarded a streetcar. It slugged along. It faced the river with beautiful homes and shops sitting like wealthy old ladies having tea on the water. A whiff of cheroot smoke and the scent of oysters swarmed Zora as she entered the most bustling area of the city. She kept her eyes down and pulled the scarf up around her neck to mask her face.

But then her skin went clammy, like someone was too close, breathing down her neck. She felt watched.

She wondered if it was just paranoia. If Mama B's warning had gotten to her.

She decided to get off one stop early.

Zora left from the back exit and stepped onto North Rampart Street. A white man also got off. Her arms prickled, turning to gooseflesh, but she didn't dare turn around. Instead, she paused to glance at a house and meandered down side streets.

The sky growled overhead with the threat of rain. Zora ducked into a flower shop, Ambrose's Arbor, right before rain rushed down the shop windows and pounded the roof like rocks thrown by a giant.

A squat white woman glanced up as the door jingled. "You can go around back."

"I'm not picking up anything. I have money. I'm looking for flowers," she said, eyes volleying between the woman and the man getting soaked outside in the rain.

The shopkeeper went back to arranging flowers in her vase. "Don't be long."

Zora looked around, increasingly panicked, inhaling scents to pass the time and calm herself. Suddenly, she stumbled upon the starshaped flower Phillip had given her months ago.

"That's a starflower," the woman said, looking up from her arrangement again. "Native to Germany."

Fire and flood left the skies above New Orleans, and the storm tapered off. She looked outside the flower shop window. The man was gone.

"You want to buy it?" the shopkeeper asked.

"Thank you, but no," Zora said.

"This is a place for buying," she snapped.

"Sorry, all right?" Zora dug money from her coin purse. "How much?"

"Not enough."

Zora apologized again even though she wanted to scream at the woman, and exited the store.

The Quarter refilled with people heading in a thousand directions. She willed herself to disappear and ran all the way back to the house. She unlocked the back door and stepped inside. "Phillip," she called out, pulling off the red shoes and taking the mirror from her satchel so she could set it on the table.

"Zora? Are you all right?" Phillip rushed in. His eyes filled with relief at the sight of her. "You weren't here, and the storm . . . I was worried."

"I'm okay," she said, pulling him into a hug. "Just had to step out." She paused, wondering how to phrase what had happened at Mama B's.

Phillip leaned his forehead against hers. "Come to the front room," he said after a moment. "I have a surprise for you."

Zora followed him, finding newspapers scattered across the table and a familiar shape lying on the floor.

"Look who was outside," he said, holding up her orange cat. "He found us!"

Zora screeched with delight. She picked the cat up and felt his buzzing purrs against her stomach.

"And they've concluded the Magnolia was a freak accident. No one was seriously injured," he continued, flipping through the papers. "They're still collecting evidence, but it's dying down."

"I can't believe—" she started to say but froze. The cat leapt from her arms.

"The window, Phillip."

The white man from the streetcar stood outside, staring in at them. Slowly, he dropped something on the stoop and walked away.

Zora waited until he was out of sight before she opened the door, her heart thumping wildly as she picked up a red envelope. There was a watermark on it that she could barely make out in the darkness. Rushing inside, she opened the letter, Phillip reading over her shoulder.

February 9, 1929

You both will suffer grave consequences if you don't turn over the mirror and shoes in your possession. Bring the objects to the Ursuline Convent at midnight.

Choose your fate wisely.
Principium et finis

In place of a signature was a symbol—a terrible crow with a two-headed snake in its mouth. She turned over the envelope, now realizing the watermark displayed the same symbol. The same as the circus with that terrifying fortune-teller.

"Mama B... That's where I was today," Zora said. "She warned me about the crow and the snake." She looked at Phillip. "They know where we are. And the ship doesn't leave for three days."

Phillip kissed her forehead. "I'll finish packing. We'll go see her. Right now."

But the stress and weight of their situation sat on her chest like a monster that would never go away.

26

ora and Phillip took a hired car back into New Orleans with Phillip's valise. The cat curled up in Zora's lap as if he knew she needed him close. They were headed to see Mama B at the conjure pharmacy on South Rampart Street and decided to go to Phillip's parents' house right after.

"The street's all blocked off. Been like this since I left the French Quarter earlier," the driver told Phillip.

"Why?" Phillip asked.

"A fire."

Zora's heart hiccuped. "Let me get out and look."

"Zora, no." Phillip put a hand on her shoulder.

She removed it. "I have a bad feeling. I'll be right back."

He nodded and directed the driver to pull over for a moment.

Zora left the car and walked around the corner to the AceJack Pharmacy. She startled backward, knocking into a woman.

"Excuse you," the white woman spat.

"I'm sorry."

Zora blinked. She couldn't believe what lay before her.

The pharmacy—which had been perfectly intact just hours earlier—smoldered. Curls of smoke rose from the side of the building. Flames scorched the bricks and climbed toward the higher windows. Shattered glass spilled onto the street.

She tried to take a step closer, but the policemen had blocked pedestrian access. She felt dizzy, and her temples ached. Inside the fiery pyre, the symbol of the crow with the two-headed snake appeared on the pharmacy's burning door.

Zora scrambled back to the car. She could barely get sentences out as she tried to tell Phillip what she'd seen. Phillip ordered the driver to take them to his parents' house.

Zora thought her pulse might never slow again.

Phillip retrieved a large key from his pocket and unlocked the front double doors of his family's home.

He tiptoed into the foyer. "Wait here."

Zora's body twitched with fear as an interior door opened and a woman stepped out.

"Is that my eloped son...finally come home to see his mother?" The woman approached, the one with the chalky skin. She was still dressed in her voluminous black.

"Mother, I want you to meet my wife," Phillip said, and he motioned for Zora to step forward with him as his mother seemed to tremble ever so slightly. She looked as if a breeze could knock her over. "Zora."

"Let me have a look at her. Come closer and into the light." Her voice creaked, perhaps from lack of use. She raised a wobbly hand, beckoning.

Zora's stomach twisted, and her skin blossomed with heat. The terror of what this white woman might say to her, how she might react about her being colored raced around inside her.

"Zora, this is my mother, Gertrude Heinrich Deveraux."

That name. She'd heard it before, from Mama B and from the white ladies at the garden party. The cursed family. *Phillip's family.*

The woman and Phillip shared the same blue eyes, though hers seemed to dart around the room like she was a rodent expecting a trap. She placed a wrinkly hand on Zora's sweaty brown cheek, and Zora tried not to flinch. "Phillip, she's colored. . . ."

"I am," Zora replied proudly. A cold sensation dropped into Zora's stomach. She braced for all manner of slurs and outrage.

"Come, let us sit."

Phillip carried their bags into a formal parlor, which was dark and dusty. Zora and Phillip perched themselves on a hard, uncomfortable sofa while his mother floated onto a ratty chair across from it. She leaned forward, examining Zora more closely.

"Well, you are something." It wasn't clear whether that was good or bad.

"She is. The love of my life," Phillip added.

She leaned close to Zora again, holding her chin and turning her face to inspect her features. More sweat appeared on Zora's forehead. "I've seen you before, in my mirror. A little girl the color of a chocolate swirl and then a young woman who sings. Age is taking my memories from me. But they shake loose sometimes."

Phillip and Zora looked at one another. The surprise etched on his face made it clear he had not heard this before.

"So you have married like you said you would," Gertrude continued. "But you've decided to come back?"

"Not exactly. We're going to Paris so we can be together. The ship leaves in three days at midnight. I need my passport. And we need someplace to stay."

She paused. "Living in Europe won't be easy right now. I'll give you money since there's probably no way of talking you out of this plan."

Phillip took his mother's hand and kissed it. "Thank you. *Thank you*." He looked at Zora. "I also need a car. For a friend."

"Ah. Well, that will need to be arranged with your father."

"Where is he?"

"He's still on business in New York. Perhaps your friend can come collect it when he gets back." She peered at their bags. "And my mirror? Did you bring that home as well?"

Phillip removed it from his satchel, his face flushing a bit.

She held it up, admiring each groove and indentation, then she placed it on her frail lap and ran her wobbly fingers over the glass surface. "It used to show me everything that was going to happen to our family. And I used it to make sure we'd always be comfortable."

"What do you mean?" Phillip asked.

"I guided your father into choosing the right sorts of business dealings and even played the lottery when I knew we'd win. My father, Cay, gave me that mirror to help protect me, to help make sure we would be all right and survive. We used it as we saw fit."

"You changed things?" Phillip said, shocked.

A pulsating worry flooded Zora. How much did they change? How much *could* you change?

"We did what we needed to survive, I suppose . . . and probably a little bit more," she admitted, looking wildly around the room again. Zora wondered if she could see things they couldn't.

Phillip pulled out the letter and gently refocused Gertrude's attention, showing her the watermarked symbol of the crow with the two-headed snake in its mouth. "Someone else knows what it can do."

His mother gazed into it. "It's the curse."

Zora leaned a little closer.

"There's a curse mixed in with our magic, and we've felt it. Babies that were born still, flooding, accidents, disease. For every two wins we had, a loss followed. It's our family's bad luck, our lot in life. Whenever I look into a mirror or a pool of water, even a drop, I see more storms, more death, more chaos."

"What should we do?" Phillip's voice held fear for the first time.

"Never use the magic again," she replied simply, not looking away from the mirror. She rubbed her fingers over it as if to say goodbye.

Phillip's mother suddenly looked up at Zora. Her eyes combed over her body. Then she placed a hand on Zora's chest. After a moment, she moved her hand to Zora's lower abdomen and nodded.

"Be careful. You're carrying precious, precious gifts. Don't let the curse take them."

27

As Zora hid out the three days at Phillip's childhood home, Mardi Gras descended upon New Orleans like the storm that had threatened the skies above for days on end. It was as if the chest of the city had been cut open to expose the sound of its heart. Rhythms and timbres and crescendos of sound vibrated through everything, its streetcars, its homes, its cobblestones, all day and all night. Every pronouncement her aunt had made had been true. She'd said, *"Mardi Gras is when the city unleashes its monsters. The masks people wear all year come off; the things they keep inside all pour out. Like the good Lord knew we needed a few nights of sin to stay on the righteous path. There will be pretty costumes and beads and king cake and drinks. More than you could ever want—or need."*

Zora wished she could go out. She wished they could enjoy the parade, could sample the steaming beignets that this city was known for. She wished she wouldn't feel like a bird trapped in a cage any longer. But she told herself that soon everything would be different. Maybe she could even write to Mama and tell her all her good news once they reached Europe. She was married to someone she deeply loved, someone she thought even her suspicious daddy might like. When she was in Paris and far, far away from any damage her magic had done, they could go back to being a family.

Thick clouds clustered overhead, roiling and rumbling with the promise of heat and rain. The air held the taste of salt and sulfur. Her skin prickled as if it felt the electricity gathering in the sky. *"Trouble,"* her mama would've said.

Phillip was in the kitchen, making their lunch, all the hired help dismissed for the next few days to give them refuge. She could hear Mrs. Deveraux puttering about upstairs, talking to herself.

Zora thought about the first time she'd visited this fortress of a house, the strange thing her magic had done to keep her safe. The strange power she hadn't achieved before or since—disguise. Could she do it again? It would certainly help if they ran into any trouble before they could get to the ship. Maybe it would be enough to protect them.

She walked over to a hand mirror resting on a table in the hallway. Peering at herself, she tried to replicate the warm, tingling feeling she had felt when she'd sneaked into the Deveraux house and somehow changed the way she looked.

Nothing.

Zora straightened. What had happened last time? She thought of the panic she'd felt at the prospect of getting caught, pictured the server who had almost seen her. She needed Phillip but wished she had Jo to help her figure this all out. She wished she could tell her about the magic, to let her into this secret part of her.

Zora willed herself to think about Jo and what she might say about that moment, about all of this, actually.

Suddenly, her stomach flipped. She gasped, almost dropping the mirror. A new face stared back at her—Jo's beautiful face. And just like that, it flickered before disappearing completely.

She tried to recapture it, the perfect sandy-brown bob, the beaded neckline of her favorite dress, her hazel eyes, the bright red lipstick she always wore. Nothing.

Zora inhaled. Her heart thudded. Her limbs buzzed with it all. The important thing was that she knew she could do it. She could use her magic to transform if she needed to. She'd use the rest of their time holed up in this place to practice.

The next night when Phillip opened the bedroom door, Zora stood holding her cat. Two simple valises sat beside her feet. She'd packed them last night. Only their essentials—the mirror, the shoes, their love letters, and a few clothes she'd gotten from Mrs. Deveraux. The rest they'd sort out when they got there.

He joined her at the window. "A penny for your thoughts?"

"Try a nickel," she said with a smile.

"I can feel your worries leaking out of you." He wrapped his arms around her waist. "I thought I told you not to fuss."

"That's like telling the sky not to rain."

He kissed her neck. "We're going to be all right. As long as we're together. We're strongest together."

Zora stared down at a side table where the letter sat, the insignia of the crow with the snake in its mouth almost staring at them. "They want the mirror and my shoes."

"They can't have them," he whispered into her ear.

"Will you fight the police, too?" She felt him squeeze her tighter.

"Everyone. Anyone who comes in our way."

Even though she wanted to fight a smile, it tucked itself into the corner of her mouth. But the worries quickly crept back in. The tickle and hum of the magic beneath her skin. She had to tell him about her new discovery. She had to show him what her magic could do now . . . in case it was another thing she'd end up not being able to control.

"I have to show you something," she said, almost whispering.

Phillip's eyebrow lifted with curiosity.

Zora glanced at the picture of his mother on his bedside table, then closed her eyes and concentrated. She held that image in her mind and took a deep breath. A warmth flickered over her, and she felt her skin flush as the disguise settled on her.

Phillip stepped backward, stumbling over his own feet. "What . . . What did you do?"

"I don't exactly know," she replied, then told him about the first night she'd tried it, when she'd sneaked into his house, and how she'd been practicing.

She caught a glimpse of herself in the mirror. The whiteness of her skin was terrifying. She could hold on to the disguise for a few minutes now, though she wasn't so keen to hold on to this one.

"Go back to being my beautiful wife," he said, mirroring her thoughts.

She took a deep breath and closed her eyes again. The warmth dissipated. Phillip touched her skin with hesitant fingers.

"It's you again," he replied. "Thank God." He checked his pocket watch. "Ready to go, Mrs. Deveraux?" he said, his blue eyes full of promise and hope. "It's an hour until midnight."

"Ready as I'll ever be."

They took a hired cab with their two valises and Zora's cat. Parades clogged the streets and made it hard to navigate the city. Drunk couples danced in the streets, children ran up and down sidewalks, lighting firecrackers, and music poured out of every corner, making the trip slower than it should have been.

What if they didn't make it on time? What if Rocco left the pier, assumed they weren't coming? What if they couldn't leave?

Phillip took her hand and kissed it. "I can hear your thoughts again. Don't worry."

The cabdriver stole glances at them in the rearview mirror, frowning.

"How can I *not*?" she whispered.

He leaned close to her ear, his bottom lip grazing her skin and leaving behind a warm trail. "Rocco will wait. In less than an hour, we'll be on a ship headed for Paris. The City of Lights."

"Seems like New Orleans is that tonight," she said. "Will you miss it?"

He took her hand again. "I have the only thing I need from New Orleans right here beside me."

The cabdriver continued to watch them as he drove them to

the dock. Zora inched closer to the window. She didn't want him to throw them out into the crowded streets. She told herself that soon she wouldn't have to worry about such things. That once in Paris, she would be able to touch and kiss her husband without fear.

Finally, they reached the harbor. Tidy lines of passengers fanned out, and shipmen collected tickets and carried valises and trunks.

Zora scanned the crowds for Rocco. How would they find him among all these people?

"Tickets out! Line up by voyage class," a man shouted.

"I don't see him," Zora replied. "They're starting to board."

Phillip jerked left. "Over there." He pointed. "Rocco! Rocco!"

They weaved left and right, slipping and sliding through the thick crush. Phillip shoved the valises forward to make a path. Some grumbled, others stared at Zora, and many fussed about them trying to cut in line. Finally, they reached where Rocco stood with Jo . . . and three other men.

Their eyes met. Jo dropped her gaze.

The biggest of the men stepped forward and took a cigar from his mouth. "We've got a problem," he said. "Your friend here owes me some money."

"And he didn't make good on his promise," another added.

"Rocco, what's this all about?" Confusion marred Phillip's face, and his eyes darted all around.

The ship bellowed. The whistle blew.

"You were supposed to give me your car," Rocco reminded him flatly. "And you didn't."

"Final passengers. All aboard," a voice shouted. "All aboard."

"I told you what happened. We had to destroy it. They were after us." Phillip's face flamed red. "I've written to my father. You can collect another one from him in a few days."

Rocco shrugged. "Too late for that. I told them you'd settle the debt now instead."

"We would what?" Zora said, the fury inside her snapping loose. "Jo, how could you let him do this?"

Jo's cheeks flushed, and tears started to pour out of her eyes.

"We're married now, too," Rocco said. "She does what I tell her to do. Like good wives should."

"How much do you owe this time, Rocco?"

"A lot," one of the men said. "He's been skimming off the top of our shipments. Dropping them off and pocketing part of the cash." The man flexed his knuckles. "Rocco says it was your idea. That you needed the cash. But I couldn't understand why the only son of Big Phillip Deveraux Senior would need money." His gaze turned to Zora. "Now I know why Mama and Daddy cut you off."

Phillip lunged forward. Two men grabbed him by the arms.

"We'll put a bullet right between your eyes unless you pay up," one snarled.

Heat raced through Zora's body. The money they'd been given was supposed to help them find a place to live in Paris, tide them over until both of them could get work.

A rumble left the ship's belly one final time.

"How could you do this?" Phillip seethed. "After all I've done for you."

"Done for *me*?" Rocco's dark eyes turned into pools of venom.

"I helped you."

Rocco laughed maniacally, then smiled at them both. "Well, I'll leave you all to it. Jo and I have to go." He yanked her toward the line of final passengers boarding the ship.

Zora stood stunned in place. Rocco and Jo were taking their tickets. They were taking their future. And they didn't even bother to look back.

28

The noise of Mardi Gras drained away. The docks and the wail of the ships. Her heartbeat bellowed in her ears. "The Fratello family is still owed their money, and it seems you're on the hook to pay," the biggest of the three men shouted at Phillip. "What do you plan to do about it?"

"I'm sure we can work something out," Phillip offered, with a tremor of worry.

Zora's anger flared.

She let her eyes close for a moment as an angry storm woke up inside her chest. The heat of it became a fireball. Electricity skated across her skin as if lightning was about to strike, while the sky growled overhead.

"We were promised a car and cash."

"A red Chrysler Imperial Eighty," one of the others chimed in.

"And a glove compartment with a thousand stacks," the second one said. "That was our deal."

"We didn't make any deal with you," Zora barked.

The biggest one's mouth cracked a sly smile. "Sweetheart, we ain't talking to you." He turned to Phillip. "Can you tell your colored broad to mind her business or we'll mind it for her?"

The heat of humiliation burned her cheeks.

Phillip pushed forward to block her. "Don't speak to her."

The big man pounded his beefy fist into Phillip's chest. "Do you know who I work for? Do you know who I am? We're not leaving until we get what we came here for."

Phillip pointed at the suitcase. "All we have are these and the clothes on our backs."

The man tsk-tsked. "That's a shame." Slowly, he lifted his gun.

Phillip lunged, trying to knock it from his hand.

Everything slowed like in a motion-picture reel, each frame stretching out and warping before the next. The pop of the gun was as if someone had ignited a firework right beside Zora's head.

"Phillip!" she screamed as the dock turned to chaos.

The whole of her transformed into pure and raw magic. It poured out of her like a great storm, the music notes spiraling into winds and torrential rain and a vortex of heat. A blinding light filled the pier, pushing through every crack and crevice in the wooden slate beneath her feet. It looked like a star had fallen from the heavens.

Then bodies hit the pier, the crash and clatter of broken bones a secondary melody, the wailing sounds of the crowd a lingering refrain.

Zora didn't know if she'd ever be able to stop.

"It's all right," Phillip panted, getting up from the ground. "I'm here."

She fell to her knees, burying her face in her hands. Sweat skated down her back.

Then she gazed up at the carnage. Two of the Fratello brothers lay dead to her left, while the third scrambled off on his hands and knees. A pile of bodies made a trail to the ship. Zora spotted both Jo and Rocco. A ribbon of blood oozed from Jo's mouth. Rocco's head was cracked open like an egg. Even though Jo had chosen Rocco, chosen to betray her and Phillip, Zora's heart still shattered.

Phillip helped Zora to her feet. Her arms and legs trembled, and she was afraid her knees might give out any second.

"What have I done?" she whispered.

"You saved me." Phillip's big blue eyes held raw fear. It was the first time she'd ever seen this look. "You have to disguise yourself. You have to make sure no one can recognize you."

"No, I can't, I can't—" Zora started. Her heart thudded wildly.

As usual, police swarmed the pier. "We have to get out of here." Zora looked around. There was only one way off the pier, and it was right beyond the cluster of policemen. "I could use my magic again."

"No," Phillip said.

She tried to walk and almost fell. Phillip held her tighter. Zora balled her hands into fists, calling the magic to her palms, trying to draw out any strength she had left inside her.

A ruddy-cheeked policeman caught sight of them, and she saw recognition dawning. "Hey!" he shouted. "You two!"

Zora opened her mouth, but no sound came out.

She heard the words *wanted* and *posters* and *fugitives*.

"Do it now," Phillip pressed, his blue eyes filling with tears. "For *me*. Then get out of here."

"I'm not leaving you." Exhaustion radiated through her; the magic in her veins spent.

"You have to, and you will." He squeezed her hands, pushed his wallet into them, then put his forehead to hers. She closed her eyes. The only image she could think of was Jo. Her anguished face flashing over and over again. The warmth of the disguise flickered over her skin.

"Don't move!" she heard a policeman shout.

Her eyes snapped open. She looked down at her arms, now almost as pale as Phillip's. He kissed her cheek, released her hand, and stepped forward.

A circle tightened around them. The policemen held up their guns and batons. The barrels of them were dark circles pulsating before Zora's exhausted eyes.

This was it.

This was her punishment.

This was how it would all end.

"She didn't do anything. I don't even know her. She's a passenger on the ship."

"Phillip!" she whispered. "Don't. Please."

One of the policemen held up the Wanted posters, Phillip's face shining back at them. "This you?"

He nodded.

"And you do all this?"

He dropped his chin and held his wrists out. "Go," he grumbled to Zora. Then to the officers: "I did this."

"No," she pleaded.

One of the policemen snatched him and restrained him.

Zora swallowed a scream while she watched Phillip being carted away.

29

three days later, Zora stood in the middle of Union Station in her red shoes. People rushed past her. The numbers flipped. Train times. Track locations.

She stared at the Empire Line, Train 2389 headed to New York City, and then down at her schedule for the Sunset Limited to San Francisco.

Zora couldn't put her family at risk. Rocco's associates, the Fratello family, would be looking for her and so would whoever sent that threatening letter. She had to truly disappear this time.

No more shows at the Petit Sapphire.

No more New Orleans.

No more Jo.

She would take the job at the Lupine and focus all her energy and efforts on Phillip's case.

The ginger bird on her shoulder cooed, and she glanced up at her once-cat. "You're going to help distract them with your beautiful voice and charming ways if anyone comes nosing around, right?"

The bird chirped back its approval.

"Then you'll turn back into my precious cat once we're on board."

The bird nodded and touched its beak to her nose.

When Phillip had been taken, it was like something had been unleashed in her, her magic pouring out in ways it never had before. She used all of it—her anguish, her grief—all the sour notes to move and transform in ways she had never thought possible before. She'd laughed bitterly, vaguely thinking of all the ways it could have helped her—could have helped *them*—before. She had made her way back to the hideout house, beyond caring about the snake and the crow, part of her almost willing them to show.

They didn't.

Now Zora took a deep breath and released her magic, buried beneath her stomach. In the ticket booth's reflection, she watched herself change—brown arms, legs, and face lightening to cream, zigzag curls lengthening to straight, full mouth thinning out to a sharp, severe line—just as she'd make a skeleton key into a butterfly under Oma's command as a child. Her skin felt hot and angry missing its color, knowing what she was doing felt like a betrayal to the very core of her.

Only for a few minutes, she told herself.

She marched up to a white man with a bushy mustache behind a ticket booth. "First-class sleeper to San Francisco," she said, placing crisp dollar bills on the ledge.

He glanced up and his brow furrowed. "For one?"

A sheen of sweat appeared on her forehead. The bird released a song, diverting his attention.

"What a lovely pet," he said. "A ruddy kingfisher, right?"

"Ah, yes, yes," Zora replied, trying to infuse confidence into her voice.

"I saw one in a magazine once. My mama loved birds. Had her own aviary." He gazed at it lovingly while handing her a ticket. "Off for a visit?"

"Yes, to see relatives," she lied.

"A beauty like you shouldn't be traveling alone."

"My husband's meeting me at the next stop." The lie made her heart feel like it might stop mid-beat.

A white porter took her trunk, and she lined up to board the first-class car. She glanced down the length of the train, where the colored cars filled, and she felt a pang of guilt. The money from Phillip's family and her magic allowed her to travel in comfort.

She wiped blood away from her nose with a handkerchief. She hadn't used her magic for this length of time, and she never would again. The disguise made her feel sick. Like she'd erased the deepest part of herself. Her hand found her stomach, and she pressed it anxiously. Stepping up the stairs and into the train, she didn't look back. If she did, she thought she might not keep going.

In the sleeper car, two modest beds were arranged in an L shape next to a porcelain washbasin and a small icebox. The brochure said it would have the best view of the Bayou country, the Mexican border, the southwestern deserts, and the California mountains passing by the window.

She tipped the porter who stared at her a little too long. "Tell them I'm not to be disturbed. If the train isn't going off the tracks, I don't want to know," she snapped, using her worst-white-lady voice.

She closed the door and let the disguise drift away. The deep brown of her skin returned; her body cooled and settled. The straight waves curled strand by strand. She set the birdcage closest to the window and opened the cage door.

Zora unclasped her suitcase and moved her bundle of love letters. She stared at a few of Phillip's clothes that she'd packed and took one of his shirts, pressing it to her nose. If only her magic could remake him here, pull him from behind those bars.

Her bird started to sing and coo until Zora's tears subsided.

"Change back, please." The bird nodded as its tiny wings turned to chubby legs and its feathery tail elongated into a furry rope. Within seconds, her beautiful cat stared back. She clenched her teeth, wiped her face, and finished unpacking.

She would be fully showing soon. Phillip would miss her pregnancy, the birth of their children, everything. She closed her eyes to keep the flood of tears inside and rubbed her belly. The train lulled her to sleep.

She was just Sadie Walker again.

She was just in her Harlem bedroom.

She was just a musician who had never stepped foot in New Orleans.

Her cat purred loudly, then licked her cheek and kneaded his paws against her shoulder.

"I'm up. I'm up. Quit your noise. I'm too weak to disguise myself right now."

A faint glow illuminated the dark compartment. Her valise was glowing. She hastily drew back the buckles. The mirror. Her heart thudded, and dread filled her.

Zora gulped and picked it up. Without thinking, she began to hum a tune—the last song she and Phillip had played together at the Petit Sapphire, the one he had hummed on their wedding night: "Moonlight." It all felt like a thousand years ago. The music notes danced in the air, then turned, hitting the glass like rain. The mirror suddenly went blank, then showed a storm. The night sky boiling, punctuated by angry stars. A flood.

A willow tree grew from the waters.

Zora lifted the mirror closer to her. Entangled in the roots of the tree was the familiar coffin. But now the shroud moved in the wind before flying off entirely.

Zora peered closer. The coffin, it appeared, was made of glass. And it was not her body that lay inside, but that of a beautiful young white woman. Her hair was golden, her face serene. It was the woman from the visions with Oma.

What was her name?

"Elva," she remembered.

Then the young woman opened her eyes. And stared back.

EPILOGUE

May 28, 1929

 San Francisco, CA

 Dear Phillip,

 The days grow long without you. The thought of you in that cell haunts me.

 I have news that I wish I could tell you face-to-face, so that I could see your beautiful eyes light up. But a letter is as close as I can get.

I've confirmed what I believe your mother suspected—I'm pregnant. With two babies.

I went to San Francisco to take the job at the Lupine. And I'm not going to stop trying to get you released. I'll sing our song to the twins every night. I'll tell them how wonderful their father is.

All my love,

Zora

ACKNOWLEDGMENTS

I'll keep it short and sweet. I'd love to thank the Hyperion team for bringing me to this project. Thank you, Brittany Rubiano, Emily Meehan, Kieran Viola, Seale Ballenger, Marci Senders, Elke Villa, Dina Sherman, Andrew Sansone, Holly Nagel, and Danielle DiMartino. This book was a wonderful challenge that stretched my creative muscle.

I've had a blast creating this series with three of the most talented writers in the game: Julie C. Dao, L. L. McKinney, and J. C. Cervantes. It's been an honor to get to create alongside you. I adore your brilliant minds. Extraordinary. Mirror squad forever.

Thank you to the readers for following us into this dark wood. . . .

Thank you to New Orleans. You're never not interesting.

AGNES'S FAMILY

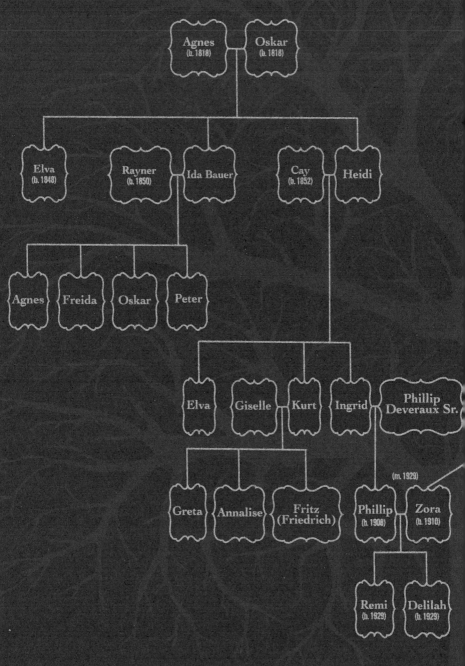